The Mystery of the
LAUGHING
SHADOW

ALFRED HITCHCOCK
and The Three Investigators in

The Mystery of the
LAUGHING
SHADOW

Text by William Arden

Based on characters created by Robert Arthur

Illustrated by Harry Kane

7490

F
ARD

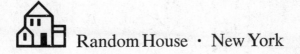

Random House · New York

This title was originally cataloged by the Library of Congress as follows:
Arden, William.   Alfred Hitchcock and the three investigators in The mystery
of the laughing shadow. Text by William Arden. Based on characters created
by Robert Arthur. Illustrated by Harry Kane. New York, Random House [1969]
178 p. illus. 22 cm. (Alfred Hitchcock mystery series, 12) 1.95   Three boys
try to solve another mystery involving a gold Indian amulet and a weird laughing shadow that appeared to them in the night.   [1. Mystery stories] I. Arthur,
Robert. II. Kane, Harry, illus. III. Title. IV. Title: The mystery of the laughing
shadow. (Series)   PZ7.A6796Aj   [Fic]   78–75885
ISBN 0-394-81492-4   0-394-91492-9 (lib. bdg.)

Library of Congress Catalog Card Number: 78-75885
Manufactured in the United States of America

Designed by Jackie Mabli

Printed and bound by Colonial Press, Clinton, Mass.

CONTENTS

A Few Words from Alfred Hitchcock vii
1. A Laugh in the Night 3
2. A Mysterious Message 7
3. Attacked! 13
4. The Devils of the Cliffs 21
5. The Chumash Hoard 27
6. Jupiter Reveals a Deception 33
7. Ghost-to-Ghost Hookup 45
8. Shapes in the Night 53
9. "Where No Man Can Find It!" 65
10. Pursuit in the Hills 75
11. Jupiter Has a Suspicion 83

12. Call the Police! 91

13. Caught! 99

14. Jupiter Has a Hunch 109

15. A Villain Unmasked 121

16. The Dark Men Appear 127

17. A Dead End 135

18. Down the Cliff 143

19. Into the Mountains 151

20. The Chumash Hoard! 163

21. Alfred Hitchcock Detects a Loose End 173

A FEW WORDS FROM ALFRED HITCHCOCK

Greetings! I am delighted to have you join me for another adventure with those three amazing lads who are known as The Three Investigators. This time a mysterious golden amulet from a lost Indian hoard leads them into more danger than you could possibly imagine. And for additional excitement, a strange laughing shadow pops up in the most unlikely places.

If you have read any of their previous cases, of course you know all about my young friends. The First Investigator, Jupiter Jones, is stocky, almost fat; Pete Crenshaw is tall and muscular, and Bob Andrews is slighter and more studious. They all live in Rocky Beach, California, a small community on the shores of the Pacific not far from glamorous Hollywood, and they make their Headquarters in a mobile home trailer cleverly hidden from sight in The Jones Salvage Yard. This unique junkyard is owned by Jupiter's aunt and uncle, with whom he lives.

But why should I bore you with further introductions. On with the case! The shadow is about to laugh —or would screech be a more appropriate word?

ALFRED HITCHCOCK

The Mystery of the
LAUGHING
SHADOW

A LAUGH IN THE NIGHT

Bob Andrews and Pete Crenshaw were still two miles from their homes in Rocky Beach when they had to turn on their bicycle lights. Darkness comes suddenly in the mountains of Southern California in the winter.

"Gosh," Pete said, "we should have started back sooner."

"The swim was worth being late." Bob grinned.

Their fine day in the mountains, topped off by a swim in a mountain stream, had been spoiled only by the absence of Jupiter Jones, the third member of their Three Investigator trio. Jupe had had to work in his Uncle Titus' salvage yard.

Tired but happy, the two boys were pedaling past a high stone wall in the mountain darkness when a thin, startling cry suddenly came out of the night.

"Help!"

Surprised, Pete squeezed his brakes, coming to an abrupt stop. Bob ran full tilt into him.

"Ooff!" Bob grunted.

Pete whispered, "Did you hear that?"

Bob untangled his bike and glanced quickly toward the wall. "Yes, I heard it. Do you suppose someone's hurt?"

While the two boys stood there, listening, something moved in the brush behind the wall.

"Help!"

This time there was no mistaking the urgency of the cry. Directly ahead of them, a heavy gate of tall iron bars topped with spearlike spikes was set into the wall. The boys did not hesitate. Dropping his bicycle, Pete ran to the iron gate. Bob, following close behind, suddenly gave a low, sharp cry:

"Owwwwww."

Something had flown over the stone wall and struck him on the arm—a small object that bounced away in the dark.

"Here it is!" Pete bent over to pick it up.

The two boys stared at the object in Pete's hand. It was a tiny, shining, metallic little statue. No more than three inches long, it resembled a weird, grinning, miniature man, his legs crossed as if he were sitting on the ground.

"What is it, Pete?"

"Don't ask me. It looks as if it had been fastened

onto something. See the loop on its head?"

"It came from behind the wall," Bob said. "Do you . . ."

The sound of heavy noises behind the wall suddenly interrupted him. Somebody was crashing through the underbrush. Then a muffled voice called:

"He threw something out. Get it!"

"I'll get it, boss," a second voice answered.

The lock of the iron gate rasped as someone struggled to unlock it. Looking around quickly, the boys discovered a thick growth of bushes close to the wall. They pushed their bikes out of sight and crouched down in hiding.

The massive gate swung slowly open on creaking hinges. Then a shadowy figure slipped through the trees at the edge of the highway. The boys held their breath and peered out through the leaves. It came closer, passed, and moved off along the road.

"Could you see who it was?" Bob whispered.

"It's too dark."

"Maybe we should give that statuette back. It looks like it could be valuable."

"I guess we . . . Watch it!"

A dark shape loomed up not ten feet from where Pete and Bob were crouching in the bushes. The boys froze, trying not to make a sound. The shadow seemed to tower above them in the night—tall, twisted, and humpbacked with a long, beaky nose and a small head that jerked about in an erratic way.

Suddenly a wild laugh shattered the darkness! It came from the tall shadow that stood so close to their hiding place. As the boys fought the panic that made them want to run, the shadow suddenly called out in an ordinary man's voice:

"Never mind. It's too dark to look now."

"Okay, boss," the other man answered from farther down the road. "I'll see if I can find it tomorrow."

The tall, humpbacked shadow with the weird head waited a moment for the other man to rejoin him. Then both men crunched through the bushes, and the iron gate creaked shut. Bob and Pete remained in their hiding place until they heard the lock turn, and the sounds of the two men faded away beyond the wall.

"Did you see that man?" Bob whispered. "The one with the funny head. And that laugh—what kind of laugh was it?"

"I don't know, and I'm not so sure I want to know," Pete said firmly.

"Let's go home and tell Jupe what happened."

"That idea I like," Pete agreed.

With their bikes, the boys made their way quietly back to the highway. As they started down the road toward Las Casitas Pass, the wild laugh split the night again behind them.

They began to pedal furiously, and didn't slow down until they came out of the pass and saw the friendly lights of Rocky Beach below.

A MYSTERIOUS MESSAGE

"It looks like solid gold!" Jupiter Jones exclaimed.

The stocky First Investigator of the trio looked like a solemn young owl as he studied the tiny statuette.

"Is it valuable, Jupe?" Bob asked.

"I would guess that it was very valuable," Jupiter pronounced, "and not just because it's gold."

"Gosh, Jupe, what's more valuable than gold?" Pete asked.

The grinning little statue glistened in Jupiter's hand. "Look at how carefully it's carved, fellows. It must have been made by a skilled craftsman, and look at the slanted eyes and feathered headdress. I think it's the work of some kind of American Indian, and quite old. I've seen things like it in museums."

The boys were gathered inside the old trailer that served as their headquarters. Because it had been damaged in an accident, Jupiter's Uncle Titus had not been able to sell it. Instead, he had given it to the boys to use for their meeting place, and the boys had piled so much junk over and around the trailer that no one knew it was there any more.

The trailer-headquarters could be entered only through various secret entrances. Inside, the boys had built a small office with desk, telephone, tape recorder and other equipment useful for their investigations. Next to the office was a tiny laboratory and a dark-room. Just about everything the boys used had come into the salvage yard as junk and had been rebuilt by them.

Bob and Pete finished telling Jupiter about the rest of their adventure in the mountains, while Jupiter continued to study the tiny statuette. At the end of their recital, Jupiter frowned thoughtfully.

"So you two think that whoever called for help also threw this statuette over the wall," Jupiter said. "Then the two men you heard caught him and came out to find the statuette."

"Sure, Jupe," Bob said.

"However, the call for help and the statuette aren't necessarily connected," Jupiter pointed out. "You're only making an assumption without actual proof."

Pete protested. "Gosh, Jupiter, it's okay to be careful investigators, but what more do you want?

We heard the cry, the statuette was thrown over the wall, those two men came after it, and one of them called the other 'boss'! It sure sounds like some kind of gang to me."

"Perhaps, Pete, but you still saw and heard nothing that actually connected the statuette with the cry for help," Jupiter insisted.

"What about that weird shadow?" Bob said quickly. "I never saw any man who looked like that shadow or laughed that way."

"Can you fellows describe the laugh?"

"It was high like a kid," Pete said.

"No, it was sort of like a woman," Bob corrected.

"It wasn't any woman. It was crazy."

"Hysterical and scared."

"A real mean laugh, nasty."

"Sort of sad, I'd say. Maybe an old man."

Jupiter listened to his fellow investigators with a puzzled expression. "Are you sure you both heard the same laugh?"

"Sure we did," Pete said lamely, "but I guess we didn't hear it the same."

"Yet you both heard it clearly, and very close." The First Investigator sighed. "I guess I'll have to hear it for myself to know what it sounded like. Are you both at least sure you heard a call for help?"

"We're sure!" Bob and Pete said in unison.

Jupiter's round face was deep in thought. "From where you say you were, and your description of the wall and gate, I'd say you must have been outside the old Sandow Estate."

Bob snapped his fingers. "Of course! The old Spanish Land Grant. More than five thousand acres!"

"It's mostly mountains, but old Miss Sandow's father had herds of cattle there a long time ago," Jupiter added.

"Don't they have cattle now?" Pete asked.

Bob shook his head. "No, Pete. I remember reading about the Sandows and their estate when I was doing some research in the library. Old Miss Sandow's father was the last one who actually worked the estate. When he died, only Miss Sandow was left, and she became a kind of hermit. My dad says she's what they call land-poor, which means she has more land than money. She lives alone out there except for a maid and a day-gardener. No one ever sees her."

Bob was the Research and Records man of the Three Investigators, and his facts were always correct about something he had looked up. Jupiter's face took on a serious expression.

"Which means that what you saw and heard tonight, fellows, is quite strange. What were those men doing on the Sandow Estate, and where did this statuette come from?"

"Maybe a gang was stealing from Miss Sandow," Pete said.

"But she doesn't have any money," Bob pointed out.

"Perhaps the estate has nothing to do with what you heard. The men might have just happened to be there," Jupiter suggested. "A little statuette like this would hardly be worth the time of any gang."

The First Investigator turned the tiny gold man over and over in his hands, staring at it as if the miniature man would somehow tell him what the boys wanted to know. Suddenly, he bent over the statuette, his eyes gleaming with excitement.

"What is it, First?" Bob said.

Jupiter was examining the statuette closely. His fingers began to push and pick at the bottom of the small figure. He pressed the statuette and twisted it and uttered a cry of triumph as the bottom of the figure flew open. Something fell to the floor.

"A secret compartment!" Pete cried.

Jupiter retrieved the small piece of paper that had fallen out of the statuette. He spread it out on the desk of the office, and Bob and Pete crowded around to examine it. Jupiter stared at the slip of paper and groaned.

"Is it a message, Jupe?" Bob asked.

The First Investigator bit his lip in frustration. "I don't know. It looks like writing all right, but I can't read it. It's in some foreign language!"

Pete and Bob stared at the ragged piece of paper.

"It isn't any language I've ever seen before, either," Jupiter added glumly.

The boys fell silent in disappointment. Bob and Pete both knew that Jupiter had some knowledge of several major languages and spoke three. If he didn't recognize the writing, what could it be? Then Bob stared more closely at the paper.

"Fe-fellows," he stammered, "that's not written in ink! It's blood!"

Jupiter examined the strange writing again, while Pete brushed uneasily at his hair.

"Bob's right," Jupiter said at last. "It is written in blood. That must mean that whoever wrote it had to do it in secret without any pen or pencil."

"He must be a prisoner," Bob decided.

"Or maybe someone who wants to break away from the gang," Pete added.

"It could be many things," Jupiter agreed, "which makes me think this is a job for The Three Investigators. The first thing we have to do is find someone to read the message."

"Who?"

"Well, we know one man who knows a lot about strange languages, and strange people," Jupiter decided.

"Alfred Hitchcock!" Pete said.

"Exactly," Jupiter declared. "It's too late tonight, but tomorrow we will call on Mr. Hitchcock and show him this message."

ATTACKED!

The next morning, the instant they had finished breakfast, Pete and Bob hurried to the salvage yard. Jupiter was already waiting there with Worthington and the gold-plated Rolls-Royce the boys had originally won the use of in a contest solved by Jupiter.

"We'll go to Mr. Hitchcock's studio first, Worthington," Jupiter instructed as the boys clambered into the big car.

"Very good, Master Jones," Worthington acknowledged. Despite their now firm friendship, the elegant chauffeur insisted on being properly correct at all times.

The boys had learned that it was never easy to get into the studio to see the famous director, so they always used the Rolls-Royce when they went to call on Mr. Hitchcock. The car was now at their permanent disposal, thanks to the financial aid of a grateful client who might not have received his rightful inheritance without the help of the Investigators. Because of their impressive car, they were passed quickly through the gates of World Studios.

"Well, my young friends, what strange events bring you to me this time?" the famous director asked from behind his mammoth desk in his private office.

The boys eagerly explained the events of the night before and described their discovery of the message inside the tiny statuette. Mr. Hitchcock listened impassively until Jupiter reached the part about the gold statuette and laid it on the director's desk.

Mr. Hitchcock's eyes sparkled as he studied the jewel-like grinning little man. "It is indeed very old, boys, as Jupiter surmised. And it is an amulet of American Indian craftsmanship without a doubt. I happened to learn a good bit about Indian crafts while filming one of our suspense stories for television. I would say that this amulet is definitely the work of our local Chumash Indians. We had one quite like it for our story."

"What's an amulet, sir?" Pete inquired.

"A magic charm, my boy, usually worn on a cord around the neck to ward off evil spirits or bring good fortune," Mr. Hitchcock explained. "That is the reason for the metal loop at the head of the figure. The

Chumash had many different kinds of such amulets."

"Gee," Pete said, "I didn't know we ever had Indians around Rocky Beach."

"Sure we did, Pete," said Bob. "I've read all about the Chumash. They were a small, peaceful tribe. They lived right on the coast here and later worked for the Spanish settlers."

"That is indeed correct," Mr. Hitchcock agreed, "but at the moment I am more interested in your laughing shadow. You say that it was tall, humpbacked, and had an oddly small head that seemed to jerk in a strange manner, and laugh wildly?"

"Yes, sir," Bob confirmed.

"You were close to this shadow, yet each of you describes the laugh quite differently. What do you make of that, young Jones?"

"I don't know, sir," Jupiter admitted, baffled.

"Nor do I, at the moment," said Mr. Hitchcock. "Now what of this message you claim dropped out of the statuette?"

Jupiter handed the piece of paper to the famous director. Mr. Hitchcock studied it closely. "Written in blood all right, by thunder! Recently, too, I should deduce from its legibility, which means that it has not been inside the amulet for long."

"Do you recognize the language, sir?" Bob asked.

"Unfortunately, no. It is not a language I have ever seen before. In fact, it doesn't even resemble any writing I have seen."

"Gosh," Pete said, "Jupiter was sure you'd know, sir."

"What do we do now?" Bob asked, crestfallen.

"Luckily, I believe I can help despite my ignorance of this language," Mr. Hitchcock declared, smiling. "I will send you boys to a friend of mine. He's a professor at the University of Southern California, and an expert on American Indian languages. He served as an advisor for our film. He lives right in Rocky Beach. My secretary will give you his address, and I shall expect to hear what progress you make."

The three boys thanked the director and stopped at his secretary's desk on the way out in order to get the professor's address. His name was Wilton J. Meeker, and he lived only a few blocks from the Jones Salvage Yard.

Jupiter instructed Worthington to take them to the professor's house and then return the Rolls-Royce to the agency. They could easily walk home.

Professor Meeker's small, white house was set back from the street. A white picket fence enclosed the thick tropical-like vegetation that surrounded the house. The boys opened the white, slatted gate and started up the brick walk toward the front door. When they were halfway up the walk, a man suddenly emerged from the thick garden vegetation directly in front of them.

"Fellows!" Bob gave a warning cry.

The man was short and very broad in the shoulders with a dark skin the color of deep-brown leather. His strong teeth gleamed white, and his eyes were black and wild. He was dressed all in white: a loose white shirt of some heavy, rough material knotted at his waist, a pair of narrow white knickers of the same rough material, and a broad white hat. His bare lower legs were brown and heavily muscled.

He held a long, wicked-looking knife!

The boys stood paralyzed on the walk as the man advanced on them with a trotting shuffle, his black eyes fierce. He waved the menacing knife and shouted at them in some strange, harsh language. Before they could make a sound or run, he was upon them.

His broad, dark hand reached out and snatched the tiny gold amulet from Jupiter's grasp. Then he turned quickly and ran into the bushes.

Stunned, the boys were unable to cry out or move for a long moment. Then Pete recovered:

"He got the amulet!"

Heedless of danger, Pete plunged into the thick bushes in pursuit. Bob and Jupiter followed close behind. They all reached the far edge of the garden just in time to see the dark man jump into a battered old car. There was a second man in the car, and it roared away the instant the man with the amulet jumped in.

"He got away!" Pete cried.

"With our statuette!" Bob wailed.

The boys looked at each other in helpless frustration. The amulet was gone! Then an angry voice spoke behind them.

THE DEVILS OF THE CLIFFS

"What's going on here!?"

A thin, stooped man with gray hair was standing behind the boys in the garden. He peered at them angrily through thick, horn-rimmed glasses.

"A man stole our amulet!" Pete blurted out.

"He had a knife!" Bob declared.

"Your amulet?" The man looked puzzled. "Ah! Then you must be the boys Alfred Hitchcock called about. The Three Investigators."

"We are, Professor," Jupiter confirmed proudly.

"And you have a problem for me? Some language you can't identify," Professor Meeker went on.

"We did have," Bob said glumly, "but that dark man stole the statuette. It's gone."

"Correction," Jupiter announced. "We still have a problem for Professor Meeker. The amulet is gone, but not the message. I took the logical precaution of carrying it separately."

Triumphantly, Jupiter handed the slip of paper to the professor.

"Amazing!" the professor cried, his eyes gleaming with excitement behind his thick glasses. "Come inside where I can study this properly."

Without another glance at the boys, Professor Meeker trotted to the house. He was so absorbed in the strange message he was holding in his hands that he almost ran into a tree. Once inside the small house, the professor waved the boys to chairs in his book-lined study and sat down at his desk to study the message.

"Yes, yes, there's no doubt about it. Absolutely amazing!" Although the professor was muttering aloud, he really seemed to be talking to himself. It was as if he had forgotten that the boys were there. "In blood, too. And fresh, quite recent. Fantastic!"

Jupiter cleared his throat. "Uh, Professor Meeker, sir, do you know what language it is?"

"Eh?" Professor Meeker looked up. "Oh, yes, yes, of course. It's Yaquali. No doubt at all. It's the Yaquali language. A fabulous people, the Yaquali. Few Indian tribes ever wrote, you know. No alphabets or vocabulary texts. But the Yaquali learned the Spanish alphabet, and Spanish missionaries compiled a dictionary for them so that they could read and write their own language."

"Are the Yaquali a local tribe like the Chumash?" Pete asked.

"Local? Like the Chumash?" Professor Meeker cried, blinking at Pete as if the Second Investigator was completely crazy. "Good heavens, no! The Chumash were quite a backward tribe. They never wrote their own language. Yaquali is entirely different from Chumash—as different as English and Chinese. The Yaquali aren't local at all."

"But they are American Indians?" Bob queried.

"Of course, although not from the United States," the professor said, and stared happily at the slip of paper again. "It's simply unbelievable to see a message written in Yaquali here in Rocky Beach. The Yaquali people rarely leave their mountains. They hate civilization."

"Er, what mountains, sir," Jupiter asked. "Where do the Yaquali live?"

"Where? . . . Why, in Mexico, of course," Professor Meeker said as if surprised that everyone didn't know. Then he smiled. "Ah, forgive me, boys. Of course you wouldn't know about the Yaquali. They're quite obscure, mainly because they shun contact with the white man and the modern world."

"Well, sir," Jupiter observed, "Mexico isn't far from here. I don't see why it should be so surprising for one of them to come to Rocky Beach."

"In the first place, young man, the Yaquali hate to

leave their homes, as I said. In the second place, they live in the most remote and rugged part of the Sierra Madre Mountains in Mexico. It is an isolated and terribly dry area called the Devil's Garden. They have a long record of shunning civilization. In fact, they became so hard to locate, and so skillful at climbing where no other men could climb, that they were often called the Devils of the Cliffs."

"Devils?" Pete shivered. "Were they so dangerous, sir?"

"Very dangerous if they were attacked. But, under normal circumstances, they are a peaceful people who wish only to be left alone. That is why they learned to climb so well, so that they could live up on their inaccessible mountains."

"Then how would a message from one of them get here?" Bob asked dubiously.

Professor Meeker rubbed at his lean jaw. "Well, I suppose it isn't so improbable. Although they are still quite remote, the Mexican government has been working with them over the last few years. Time and the needs of the modern world may have caught up with the Yaquali. They are an intelligent people, and they have long been in demand for their climbing skill."

"You think some of them may have come here to work?" Jupiter asked.

"It's possible, although I haven't heard of any of them being anywhere in the United States. And I can't really imagine what they would be doing in Rocky Beach. You did say that you found the message here in Rocky Beach, didn't you?"

"Yes, sir, in a secret compartment in the amulet."

"Ah, yes, the Yaquali are fond of amulets."

"But Mr. Hitchcock thought the amulet was the work of the local Chumash tribe," Bob explained. "He said it was like one you used in the television show."

"Chumash, eh. Well, that seems odd. I fail to see any connection between the extinct Chumash and the Yaquali. It's unlikely that Chumash work would have ever reached the Yaquali in Mexico. And you say that it was this amulet that the dark man stole from you?"

"Yes, sir," Pete said.

"It was solid gold, too," Bob added.

Professor Meeker stared at the boys. "Gold? A Chumash amulet? That's quite impossible, boys."

"Oh, no, sir," Jupiter declared firmly. "I examined it closely. I am certain it was gold."

"You must be mistaken, young man."

Jupiter shook his head. "I really know gold, sir."

"Mr. Hitchcock said it was solid gold, too, Professor Meeker," Bob stated.

The professor seemed stunned. His mouth dropped open, then snapped shut. He rubbed his jaw and stared hard at the boys, his eyes narrowed in thought. Then, slowly, he leaned forward.

"If it was truly gold, my young friends, you may

have stumbled onto something of the utmost im-
portance," the professor said carefully, pausing in
order to give emphasis to his words. "You may have
found a clue to a mystery that is almost two hundred
years old."

Jupiter's eyes opened wide. "A two-hundred-year-
old mystery?"

"Yes, my boy, the mystery of the Chumash Hoard!"

THE CHUMASH HOARD

"You see, boys," Professor Meeker went on, "the Chumash never used gold! There was no gold in this part of the state. If that amulet was gold, it must have come from the Chumash Hoard."

"What is it, sir? The Chumash Hoard?" Bob asked.

"Between 1790 and about 1820," the professor explained, "there was a renegade band of very dangerous Chumash in the mountains. Although there were few of them, they were deadly when defending themselves and expert at hiding. The Spanish were unable to control them, so they tried to bribe them with gold to leave the settlers alone. The band soon learned the value of gold, and when the Spanish didn't give them as much as they wanted they stole more anywhere they could find it.

"By the time they were finally beaten and their last leader, Magnus Verde, mortally wounded and captured, they were reputed to have amassed a great hoard of gold articles—jewelry and bullion. Magnus Verde refused to tell where the Hoard was hidden. All he said before he died was that no man would ever find it. The rest of the renegades vanished and were never seen again. Since then many, many men have looked for the treasure without any success. I have always thought that it was thrown into some impenetrable place—perhaps the ocean—to keep the white men from ever finding it."

Jupiter's eyes seemed to be looking far away. "I think it would have been hard for them to throw away the gold after fighting so hard to get it."

"You may be right," the professor said. "And if you have actually seen a Chumash amulet made of gold, there is good reason for thinking the Chumash Hoard does still exist somewhere. What an exciting discovery!"

"Perhaps the message says something about the Hoard," Jupiter said eagerly.

"Message?" Professor Meeker blinked again. Then he looked down at the slip of paper. "Goodness me, I forgot all about it. Of course! It may tell us."

The professor frowned as he studied the message. "Primitive languages are often hard to translate exactly because the writers think in a primitive manner. But as nearly as I can make out, it says:

'Words smoke. Sing death song. Brothers help.' I'm afraid, that's all."

"But it is a call for help?" Jupiter asked.

"I would say so," the professor agreed and stared at the message with a puzzled expression. "But I can't understand what a Yaquali message would be doing in a Chumash amulet. It's really a mystery."

"A mystery we hope to solve, sir," Jupiter pronounced somewhat pompously.

"Of course, my boy." The professor smiled. "And when you do, I shall be most grateful if you will allow me to examine the Chumash Hoard."

Professor Meeker insisted on seeing the boys as far as the gate, peering in all directions in the sunny morning to be sure that the dark man had not returned. As soon as they were by themselves again, Bob and Pete crowded around Jupiter.

"Gosh, Jupe!" Bob exclaimed. "Do you think someone has found the Chumash Hoard?"

"And someone else is trying to steal it?" Pete added.

"Maybe the amulet is a clue to where the treasure is, and someone is trying to steal it to find the Hoard!"

"Maybe it's a gang of Indians robbing Miss Sandow!" Pete's imagination began to run wild.

"That dark man sure looked like some kind of Indian."

"That laughing shadow could have been a wild Indian!"

Jupiter, his round and deceptively innocent face

deep in concentration while his companions chattered, suddenly stopped short. "Speculation won't get us anywhere now," the First Investigator declared decisively. "We must go to the Sandow Estate and see what we can find out."

"Under cover, Jupe?" Pete said. "You mean we should snoop around?"

"No, we must get into the house and talk to Miss Sandow herself. She might know something vital or have seen something. The problem is—how do we get into her house?"

As they neared the salvage yard they decided that the best way was to have Bob's dad call Miss Sandow and ask if they could visit the estate as part of a research project on Spanish land grants for their California history class. Hans or Konrad, the stolid Bavarian helpers of Uncle Titus Jones, could drive them.

"Most adults will help boys if they think it's for some school work," Jupiter observed.

Bob agreed, but Pete was looking ahead to the entrance to the salvage yard.

"Look," Pete hissed, "there's Skinny Norris!"

Sure enough, their old enemy—a tall, skinny boy with a long nose—was leaning against the entrance with his back to them. E. Skinner Norris, Skinny to the boys, hated the Investigators, and spent a good deal of time trying to prove he was smarter than Jupiter. He always failed, but since he had a large allowance and could drive a car because his father was a legal resident of another state where Skinny could get a driver's license, he was in a position to be annoying to the boys.

"Now what's he doing here?" Bob wanted to know.

"I don't expect he's come to help us," Jupiter observed wryly. "Come on, fellows, we'll go in through Red Gate Rover."

They turned and walked quickly toward the rear of the salvage yard. Out of Skinny's sight, they hurried past the back fence, which was painted with a dramatic scene of the San Francisco fire of 1906. Fifty feet from the corner, a little dog sat in the painting near a red spout of flame. They had named the dog Rover, and one of his eyes was a knot in the wood. They carefully pulled it out and reached in to release a catch. Three boards in the fence swung up, and they slipped inside the yard.

Once inside, unobserved, they crawled beneath piles of junk and through hidden passages and finally stood before a panel that opened and admitted them into their trailer headquarters. In the office they quickly discussed just what they would say to Bob's dad, and Bob reached for the telephone.

"Jupiter Jones!" a powerful female voice called from somewhere outside.

"Uh!" Pete grunted. "It's your Aunt Mathilda, Jupe. I hope she doesn't want you to work all afternoon!"

Before the First Investigator could comment, his aunt's voice boomed out again:

"Jupiter! Sakes and goodness, where does that boy get to? Jupiter! There's someone here to see you, you young scamp! A Mister Sandow! . . . Jupiter?"

The boys gaped at each other. A Mr. Sandow had come to them! Just when they were working out a scheme to get into the Sandow Estate. But—who could this Mr. Sandow be?

"Miss Sandow lives alone!" Bob remembered.

"Come on, fellows," Jupiter said, leading the way through Tunnel Two, into his workshop and the salvage yard.

JUPITER REVEALS
A DECEPTION

"Well, there you are!"

Aunt Mathilda surveyed the boys with a severe expression. "Sometimes I think this salvage yard was built just for you three to hide in!"

A tall, slender boy only a few years older than the three friends stood beside Aunt Mathilda. His dark hair was rather long, and his gray suit had a slim, foreign cut. He grinned at the boys and held out his hand:

"Hello, chaps, I'm Ted Sandow."

Concealing their intense curiosity at the coincidence of Ted Sandow's appearance in the salvage yard, the boys all shook hands with him, and Jupiter assumed his most innocent manner.

"I'm Jupiter Jones." The First Investigator introduced himself. "And this is Bob Andrews and Pete Crenshaw."

"I say, I'm pleased to meet you fellows." Ted beamed at the boys. "Friends of yours told me you were most interesting to get to know. Chap named Skinner Norris."

"Skinny Norris sent you?" Pete blurted out, amazed.

"Said I'd find you unusual, to be exact. Are you unusual? I'm most eager to meet some unusual American boys. Haven't had much chance, you see, out there on the estate."

"You're not American, Ted, are you?" Bob asked.

"I'm from England—Cambridge, to be exact. I'm visiting my Great-Aunt Sarah at the Sandow Estate. Actually, I didn't know I had a great-aunt until my father died a few months ago! My grandfather, Aunt Sarah's brother, was killed in France before my father was born. Apparently, my father got in touch with Aunt Sarah when he realized that he didn't have long to live. She sent a note, and here I am."

The tall boy grinned the whole time he was talking. Ted was obviously an eager talker. He spoke very fast, the way many Englishmen do, and his accent wasn't easy to follow. Before the boys could get in a word, he was off again:

"Well, Aunt Sarah has this barn full of old junk from years back. She's decided to house-clean and noods it all carted away. I suggested she sell it to a salvage man. She thought that a capital idea and charged me with locating one. I saw the name of your yard, but I don't know your city, so I contacted Aunt Sarah's lawyer. He lives in Los Angeles, so he told me to contact the son of a friend of his, Skinner Norris. I did, and Norris brought me here. He refused to come in himself, though. Rather odd, I thought."

Before the boys had a chance to tell Ted that it wasn't at all odd that Skinny wouldn't come into the salvage yard, Aunt Mathilda spoke up. Her sharp eyes had shown great interest at the first mention of a barn full of old junk.

"Why, we'd be glad to look at what your aunt has in her barn, Ted. When would you want us to come?"

"Right now would be excellent," Ted declared.

Aunt Mathilda shook her head. "My husband, Titus, is away at the moment. I'm afraid I can't leave the yard untended. Of course, Jupiter knows what we buy as well as I do. He could go out there after he has his lunch."

"Why don't all you boys come?" Ted said quickly.

"Konrad could drive us in the small truck," Jupiter suggested.

"I say, that would be wonderful!" Ted exclaimed. "The boys and I could talk. I've learned so little about America."

Aunt Mathilda, who was always on the lookout for

items for the yard, was soon persuaded. The boys ate quickly, then located Konrad. In a very short time they were all in the truck, following Ted's small sports car. Ted had looked for Skinny Norris to thank him, but Skinny was nowhere in sight. He had vanished completely. This surprised the English boy, but it didn't surprise the investigators at all.

"I wonder what Skinny's up to?" Pete said in the truck.

"One of his usual attempts to confound us, I presume," Jupiter answered. "I'm not worried about Skinny. But I *am* wondering why Ted happened to show up at the salvage yard the day after you fellows picked up that amulet."

"You think he knows we found the amulet, but doesn't know it was stolen from us?" Bob asked.

"Gosh!" Pete said. "That would mean there's more than one group mixed up in this!"

"Or perhaps he knows the message was removed from the amulet, and wants to get hold of it," Jupiter suggested.

"Gee," Bob protested, "he seems like too nice a fellow, Jupe."

"Perhaps it is only a coincidence," Jupiter conceded, "but I suggest we be alert, watch what we say, and keep our eyes open."

Bob and Pete agreed quickly. Meanwhile the truck, which was out of Rocky Beach by now, followed Ted Sandow's sports car into the mountains.

They drove up the winding road to the top of the pass and soon turned in at the big iron gates of the Sandow Estate, where Bob and Pete had heard the laughing shadow the previous night.

Beyond the gates and the high wall, they drove along a narrow macadam road for about a half-mile until they saw the Sandow house. It was a big, Spanish-style mansion with white walls and a gleaming red-tile roof. There were bars on many windows and small balconies in front of some on the second floor. Wrought-iron work was all over the house. But the iron was in bad repair, the white walls were cracked and dingy, and the whole house looked badly neglected.

Ted led them directly to a low, adobe barn behind the house. Inside, they found a great jumble of furniture, bric a brac, household items of the past, and some things they couldn't even name. There was so much dust on everything that it seemed as if nothing had been touched for at least fifty years.

"Aunt Sarah seems to have been something of a hermit, chaps," Ted observed. "I'm sure she has no idea what's here."

Jupiter, who loved old junk as much as his Uncle Titus, looked at the mounds of forgotten relics in awe. "It's a bonanza! Look at that spinning wheel! And that old lap writing desk for travelers."

For an hour the boys picked happily over the great, dusty piles, completely forgetting the amulet, the

Chumash Hoard, and the weird laughing shadow. Then, at last, Jupiter gave up and stood back looking at the piles.

"Uncle Titus is going to want just about all of it, and we haven't even made a dent."

"Why not come up to the house, then," Ted suggested. "We'll have some lemonade and biscuits, and you can talk to Aunt Sarah."

Bob and Pete, remembering their real reason for wanting to come to the Sandow Estate, nodded quickly and looked at Jupiter. This was just what they wanted, but no one would have guessed it from seeing Jupiter's impassive face.

"That sounds fine, Ted," the First Investigator agreed. "Konrad can start making a partial list of what's here."

"I'll send a beer out for him," Ted said.

"A beer is good." The big, blond Bavarian grinned.

Inside the big house, the boys were taken into a cool, informal room with dark, antique Spanish furniture. Ted went to ask the maid to bring the lemonade. When he came back, he was with a bird-like woman whose hands fluttered up to her neat white hair. Her pale eyes lit up with pleasure.

"I'm Sarah Sandow. I'm so glad to see that Theodore has found friends. He tells me you're from the salvage yard. I want to dispose of everything. I've been letting things accumulate for far too long."

"Yes, ma'am," Jupiter said, as Bob and Pete nodded.

"Now that Theodore is here I'm beginning to take an interest in things again. The estate is in dreadful disrepair."

The maid brought in the lemonade and biscuits, and Miss Sandow served them herself. She seemed happy to have the boys in the house.

"After last night," she explained, as the boys began to eat, "Ted convinced me that it wasn't safe to have all those things lying out in the barn."

The boys tensed, and Jupiter said, "Last night, ma'am?"

"A gold statuette was stolen. From under our noses," Miss Sandow said indignantly. "It was one of two which my poor brother Mark left behind when he had to run away. They were all I had of Mark's."

"It was really my fault, chaps," Ted explained. "You see, my dad had mentioned that my grandfather had told him about two little gold statues. I found them lying forgotten at the bottom of a drawer and was examining them in the library. I left the library, and when I came back one of them was gone."

"You don't know who took it?" Jupiter asked.

"We know it was some boy. Mr. Harris saw him."

"That I did, boys," said a deep voice from the direction of the door.

The boys turned and saw a healthy-looking man in a bright sports jacket and Bermuda shorts that displayed his long, knobby legs. His gray eyes had a twinkle in them. His hair was sandy-colored, and a small scar on his ruddy face gave him a perpetual smile.

Ted introduced them, explaining that Mr. Harris was a friend of his Aunt Sarah's.

"Interested in our robbery, are you, boys?" Mr. Harris asked with a smile. He spoke with an English accent that was somehow different from Ted's. It sounded to Jupiter like a slightly Cockney accent.

"Saw a boy running from the house and chased him to the gates. When I got there, though, I couldn't find him. He must have had friends. So I suppose we've seen the last of that statuette."

"Perhaps we could help, sir," Jupiter said quietly. "We have had some success in recovering lost and stolen articles."

"And solving mysteries, too," Pete declared.

Mr. Harris laughed. "You sound like detectives."

"Yes, sir," Jupiter said. "We are, in a small way. This is our card."

Jupiter handed Mr. Harris one of their large business cards which read:

THE THREE INVESTIGATORS
"We Investigate Anything"
?   ?   ?

First Investigator . . . Jupiter Jones
Second Investigator . . . Peter Crenshaw
Records and Research . . . Bob Andrews

Mr. Harris laughed. "Well, now, perhaps you could get Miss Sandow's statuette back. Detectives, by jove, and you have solved mysteries?"

"We sure have!" Pete exclaimed. "Chief Reynolds of the Rocky Beach police even made us deputies."

"Did he indeed?" Mr. Harris grinned, looking at the card in his hand.

From his chair across the room, Ted asked, "What are the question marks for, fellows? You don't question your abilities, do you?"

"The question marks are our symbol," Jupiter explained, looking toward Ted with a frown. "They stand for all the mysteries we attempt to solve. Sort of a trademark."

"That's great," Ted said with enthusiasm. "Let the boys try, Aunt Sarah, and I'll work with them!"

"But, Theodore," Miss Sandow objected. "There may be a gang of thieves. Would it be safe for boys?"

"Miss Sandow is right," Mr. Harris said. "Robbery is not a matter for boys."

"We're always careful, ma'am," Jupiter said, "and we would go to Chief Reynolds if we found anything serious. If it was a boy who took the statue, we might be in a good position to help. We've found that boys are often less afraid of other boys. All we would do is try to locate the statuette."

"There, Aunt Sarah," Ted declared. "You can see that the boys are responsible, and Chief Reynolds trusts them."

"Well," Miss Sandow said doubtfully. "I suppose it is rather a minor matter to take to the police directly."

Mr. Harris became serious. "The police do have too

much to do to look for a trinket without any evidence as to where it is. Possibly these boys could try to find out what did happen to it and then inform the police. If they promised to be very careful."

"Oh, they will!" Ted cried. "I say, why not offer a reward, Aunt Sarah? The boys will deserve it if they find the statuette."

Miss Sandow smiled at Ted. "Well, as long as you all promise to do nothing at all dangerous. If you do find it, I will certainly be glad to give you a reward. Suppose we say fifty dollars."

"Then it's settled," Ted said. "Smashing! Can you come for lunch tomorrow so we can plan our work?"

"I'm not sure the boys would enjoy our lunch," Mr. Harris said hastily. "Miss Sandow and I are vegetarians, boys. We eat only vegetables. I happen to be president of the Vegetarian League. Miss Sandow has given me great assistance getting our League started in Rocky Beach. You must attend a lecture. I'm giving one this afternoon as a matter of fact."

"We'd like to, sir," Jupiter said, "but now we better go back and help Konrad. My uncle will be anxious to know what Miss Sandow has to sell. We won't be able to start looking for the statuette until later."

"I'll help you," Ted said. "And don't forget the reward. Aunt Sarah won't even ask where you found the statue."

"No questions asked, eh, boys?" Mr. Harris laughed.

The boys excused themselves and went to rejoin Konrad.

Inside the barn Jupiter looked around to see if they were alone, then drew Bob and Pete into the shadows.

"Did either of you notice it?" Jupiter demanded with a grim look on his face.

"Notice what, Jupe?" Pete asked.

"Ted asked about the question marks on our card."

"People always ask, Jupe," Bob said.

"But Ted hadn't seen our card when he asked!"

Bob blinked. "You're right! Harris had the card!"

"You mean he knew about us all the time?" Pete said.

Jupiter nodded. "He knew about our card, which means he was lying to us. He didn't have to talk to *us* about selling the junk. If that was all he really came to the yard for, he could have talked just to Aunt Mathilda. Fellows, the junk was just an excuse to meet *us!*"

GHOST-TO-GHOST HOOKUP

"But how did he know about our card?" Pete wondered.

"Skinny must have told him," Bob said.

"No," Jupiter said emphatically. "He knew about us before he went to Skinny, I'm sure of that. Skinny wouldn't have told him about our card, he's too jealous of us. Anyway, if he'd learned about The Three Investigators from Skinny, he would have said so."

"And he didn't!" Bob was beginning to understand. "He pretended he didn't know we were investigators, not before we told him."

"You mean," Pete said, "that he'd found out who we were but didn't want us to know he knew?"

"But why?" Bob asked. "What reason could he

have for not wanting us to know he'd seen our card? He *came* to us."

Jupiter pondered the question. "There could only be one reason, fellows. It must be that the *way* he found out reveals something that he doesn't want us to know." Suddenly the First Investigator frowned. "Fellows, do you both have all your cards?"

Bob and Pete searched their pockets where they always carried a few of the cards. Pete exclaimed: "One of mine is missing! I'm sure I had five."

"I bet you dropped one near the gate last night," Bob said. "You probably did it when you pulled out your handkerchief to wrap up the amulet."

"And Ted found it," Jupiter added. "That means he must have been there! But he didn't want us to know!"

"Gosh," Pete said, "do you think *he* stole the amulet?"

"Perhaps, Pete," Jupiter said ominously.

"But, Jupe," Bob objected, "why would he want to hire us if he's the one who stole it? I mean, Ted was the one who persuaded Miss Sandow to hire us. He pushed hard for us."

"Maybe too hard," Jupiter observed. "He almost forced his aunt to hire us. Look, fellows, he must suspect that we have the amulet. He wants it back. That reward was his idea, and he made a point of saying no questions will be asked about where we found it if we turn it over. He's inviting us to return it for the reward."

"How would that help him?" Bob pointed out. "We'd give it to Miss Sandow. Why didn't he come to us in private? He could have."

Jupiter looked annoyed. "I admit I'm baffled about that. But two things are sure now: first, Ted wants the amulet; and second, his getting it back is much more important than any value it has."

Pete groaned. "And we've lost it. There's no way we can get it back."

"But maybe there is," Jupiter said. "I've been thinking about that ever since the man stole it. With his unusual appearance and clothes he'll have a hard time hiding in Rocky Beach. He should be easy to spot. We'll just use a Ghost-to-Ghost Hookup!"

"Sure!" Pete looked enthusiastic again.

"He should be easy for kids to find," Bob said.

"Let's help Konrad and get home fast," Jupiter suggested.

An hour later they had listed everything they thought Uncle Titus might want, and were on their way home. They reported to Aunt Mathilda, who was so fascinated by the list of Miss Sandow's junk that she never noticed the boys slip away to their headquarters. Once inside the hidden trailer, they went to work setting up the Ghost-to-Ghost Hookup.

This was the name Jupiter had given to a method he had devised for locating someone through using all the kids in Rocky Beach, or the whole area if necessary. It was a brilliant scheme because it was so simple. The boys simply called all their friends and asked for the information they wanted. If their friends couldn't answer, the friends then called *their* friends who were not known to the investigators. In this way, they could contact every kid in the area in almost no time.

The Three Investigators prepared their description of the man in white and his battered car, mentioning the fact that another man had been with him, and then called their friends. They left the telephone number of their headquarters and asked anyone who saw the men or the car to contact them at once. Within an hour nearly every boy and girl in Rocky Beach would be looking for the dark man.

"Now," Jupiter grinned, "we wait."

But by six o'clock not one call had come in, and the boys looked at each other in glum surprise. Not one kid in Rocky Beach even thought he had seen the strangers.

"They must be hiding," Bob said.

"If they're in Rocky Beach at all," Pete said.

"I'm sure they are," Jupiter insisted. "The Ghost-to-Ghost Hookup just takes time. We'll hear, but meanwhile . . ."

"Meanwhile," Pete said, looking at the clock, "we better get home for dinner."

Jupiter sighed unhappily. The limitations of being a boy sometimes made the stocky leader of the trio squirm. But he, too, would soon have to appear for his dinner.

"All right," the First Investigator agreed, "but after dinner, Bob, you go to the library and find out all you can about the Chumash Hoard. The library has a special collection of local histories, and we need to know everything about the Hoard. Also, look up Miss Sandow's brother."

"Don't tell me what I'm going to do!" Pete exclaimed.

"You," Jupiter said with determination, "are going to go back out to the Sandow Estate with me. Something is going on out there, and I want to know what it is."

"But, Jupe, what can we learn out there?" Pete wanted to know.

"For one thing," the First Investigator said, "we can try to find that laughing shadow again!"

Pete wailed, "Do we have to?"

"Be back here as soon as you can," Jupiter said firmly, ignoring Pete's wail. "And dress in dark clothes."

The sun was going down behind the high mountains to the west when Pete and Jupiter reached the iron gates of the estate. They hid their bikes in a grove of trees, and Jupiter took a small, bulging sack from his luggage carrier.

"The wall is too high to climb," Jupiter whispered, "and it runs around the whole estate on the highway side, so I came prepared."

Bending over to open up his bag, he took out two of

the small, homemade walkie-talkies he had built for the trio, and a rope with a large, four-pronged hook at the end.

"The walkie-talkies are in case we become separated," he explained, "and the rope has a grappling hook on it. I found four of them in a batch Uncle Titus bought recently."

Jupiter threw the hook up to the top of the wall, where it caught on the stone ridge. The two boys tested it, and Pete pulled himself up. At the top he peered over. Then he hauled Jupiter up. They reversed the grappling hook, and lowered themselves down inside the wall. Jupiter returned the rope to the bag, which he hid.

"We'll go up to the house," the First Investigator whispered in the fading twilight. "Be alert, Pete."

They made their way through the trees and brush to a small rise from where they could watch the house and barn. The estate grounds became dark and quiet as the last rays of sunlight vanished. There was light inside the big house, and shadows moved, but no one came out. All was quiet. In the distance they could hear cars passing on the highway.

The boys became stiff and cramped from lying so long in one position. Pete's leg went to sleep, and he moved to start the circulation. But Jupiter remained absolutely still. The lights went out downstairs in the house, and the moonless night grew even darker.

Suddenly, Jupiter touched Pete.

"What?" Pete whispered, startled.

"There!"

A vague, tall shape moved near the house. The shadow hesitated for a time as if listening, then began to move past the barn toward the woods to the east.

"When he reaches the woods, we'll . . ." Jupiter began.

The First Investigator never finished. At that moment a wild, chilling laugh echoed through the dark night.

SHAPES IN THE NIGHT

The laugh seemed to fill the dark night—high and crazy like a wild hyena.

"It must be him!" Pete whispered. "The laughing shadow! But he looks different somehow."

"What do you mean?"

"He's not so humpbacked-looking," Pete explained. "But that laugh sure sounded like him."

"We'd better hurry!" Jupiter warned. "We might lose him."

Quickly they left the small rise and headed toward the woods. The shadowy figure had taken a path that led through the trees. The boys followed behind as close as they dared. Fortunately the man never paused or looked back. He kept walking steadily ahead at a rapid pace. The wild laugh had stopped for the time being.

For more than a mile, according to Pete's estimate, the shadowy figure walked east, deeper into the forest. Then he turned off the main path into a smaller side path which led down into a small, bowl-shaped valley. There was a dirt road in the valley, and a low, rambling house built of logs. The house had a porch all around, shuttered windows, and a stone chimney.

"Some kind of hunting lodge," Jupiter whispered.

"Look!" Pete hissed.

A large, dark, oblong shape was moving along the road toward the lodge. As it drew closer, they saw that it was a truck with its lights out. The truck glided to a stop beside the man they had been following. A second man, short and heavy, jumped from the cab of the truck. There was a brief, whispered conversation in front of the lodge, then the short man went to the rear of the truck and lowered the tailgate.

Four more shadowy figures climbed down from the rear of the truck. The short man herded them into a line and pushed them toward the lodge. The taller man turned on a porch light, and the four newcomers stepped onto the porch, passing through the front door in single file.

"Yikes!" Pete whispered.

In their brief passage through the light, the four figures had, for a moment, stood out sharply—four small shapes that had no heads!

"Where . . . where are their heads?" Pete's voice quavered.

Even Jupiter was at a loss for words. "I . . . I don't know. They . . . they look like headless midgets!"

The two investigators stared at each other in the darkness.

"What's going on around here?" Pete said.

"I don't know," Jupiter answered, visibly shaken by the sight of the four headless shapes. "If we could just get closer maybe we could look through one of the windows."

The boys stared down at the lodge, which was now lighted inside, trying to decide how to approach closer.

Suddenly a wild, eerie laugh burst out of the night almost beside them. Without stopping to think what they were doing, both boys headed up the path as fast as they could go!

While Pete and Jupiter were running madly through the trees and bushes of the Sandow Estate, Bob was leaving the town library, excited by the results of his research.

He hurried to headquarters. His fellow investigators were not there, however, so he left a message for them to call him.

When he got home his dad was listening to a local news broadcast. Because Mr. Andrews worked on a Los Angeles newspaper, he never missed the news reports if he could help it. Bob went on into the kitchen, where his mother gave him some milk and cookies.

"Did you find what you wanted at the library?" Mrs. Andrews asked.

"I sure did, Mom, but Pete and Jupe are still out."

His father came into the kitchen, looking unusually upset. "I don't know what the world's coming to," Mr. Andrews said. "I just heard a report that a man was attacked in Rocky Beach this afternoon right in a public meeting hall!"

"In Rocky Beach?" Mrs. Andrews exclaimed. "How awful."

"Some fanatics, probably. The man who was attacked was the president of some vegetarian league. He was giving a lecture when two men in odd, white clothes attacked him right on the platform. Two dark men, the newscaster said."

Bob almost choked on his milk. "Dark men, Dad?"

"So it says."

"Was he hurt?" Mrs. Andrews asked.

"Apparently not, but the two men got away."

Bob said quickly, "What was his name, Dad?"

"Whose name?"

"That man who was attacked. The vegetarian."

"Let me see," Mr. Andrews said, scratching his head. "I think it was Harris. Albert Harris. They said he was president of the Vegetarian League."

It was apparent to Bob that Mr. Harris had been attacked by the same men who had stolen the amulet from Jupiter. While his parents went on talking about the outrageous attack, Bob quickly finished his milk and slipped out of the kitchen. He hurried to the telephone. One thing was certain—whoever those dark men were, and whatever they wanted, the amulet alone wasn't the whole answer.

He let the telephone ring and ring at headquarters. But Pete and Jupiter were still not back.

Pete and Jupiter crouched low in a grove of trees far from the lodge where the wild, shrieking laughter had startled the wits out of them. They were weak from running, scratched by branches and falls over roots, and shaken by their narrow escape.

Pete peered back through the night. "Do you see anything, Jupe?"

"No, I think we're safe now."

"I don't feel safe," Pete muttered. "What were those things? Midgets without heads?"

"There must be some simple explanation," Jupiter said nervously. "We didn't really get a good look. Maybe if we went back and looked in at a window . . ."

"Oh, no we don't!" Pete cried. "Not with that laughing shadow on the loose."

Jupiter sighed. "I suppose you're right. I didn't see him around, though, when we heard that last laugh."

"Who needs to," Pete said. "I vote we get out of here —fast!"

Jupe was quiet for a moment, apparently in deep

thought. Pete waited anxiously for his decision.

"Somehow, I feel sure that the dark men and the laughing shadow are part of the same mystery, Pete."

"Sure, but how?"

"That we have to uncover," Jupiter said. "But right now I agree that it would be best for us to go home."

"That's what I like to hear!"

Grinning, Pete led them across the rugged country of the estate toward the distant highway. They avoided the holes and gullies this time, but their progress was slow in the dark. Finally they reached the wall and walked along it until they came to where the bag was concealed.

Jupiter threw the grappling hook to the top of the wall, but this time it failed to catch hold on the first two tries. Pete took over for the third throw. It caught, and Pete was testing the hold when from the direction of the estate road they heard the sound of a rifle bolt snicking home!

"Come out of there, you two!"

A figure stood in the road. A tall shadow that held a rifle aimed straight at the boys.

There was nothing they could do. The two boys stepped out of the trees and bushes into the private road. Then Jupiter suddenly smiled:

"Ted! It's Jupiter Jones and Pete Crenshaw!"

Ted Sandow did not smile, and he didn't lower his rifle. Instead, the tall English boy watched the two investigators with suspicion.

"What are you doing here?" Ted asked coldly.

Pete protested. "Ted, it's us! We're working for your aunt."

"At this hour?" Ted snapped. "In the dark, sneaking around? You didn't say anything about coming back here to snoop. Where have you been on the estate?"

"Looking around. We thought the amulet might have been lost near the gate, or perhaps the thief would return in the dark," Jupiter explained glibly. "We do have your aunt's permission to try to find the statuette."

Ted hesitated. "I don't know if I should believe you."

"What about us believing you!" Pete blurted out. "You knew we were investigators all along! You found our card!"

Jupiter tried to stop Pete with a kick on the leg, but it was too late. Ted Sandow stared at Pete:

"How did you know that?"

Pete told the English boy about his slip in mentioning the question marks before he had, supposedly, even seen one of their cards. Ted looked rather chagrined, but at the same time it was clear that he admired the boys' keen thinking.

"I say," Ted exclaimed, "that was clever of you!" He smiled and lowered the rifle. "Yes, I found your card near the gate, you see. I told Mr. Harris, but he said that your card might be just a coincidence, that I should proceed with care because I could be wrong. So I asked Aunt Sarah's lawyer if he knew any boys in Rocky Beach who called themselves The Three Investigators, and he sent me to Skinner Norris, as I said. That was how I found out about you boys and the salvage yard and thought up the idea of approaching you with the offer of Aunt Sarah's junk. That's the true story, I'm afraid."

Pete suddenly understood. "You thought we were the thieves who had stolen the statuette!"

"I guess I did, fellows," Ted admitted. "I told Mr. Harris, but he wasn't sure. He suggested that perhaps the real thief had lost the statuette, and you boys had simply found it. So we decided to get you out here, offer a reward, and maybe persuade you to return it under the pretext that you had succeeded in finding it."

Jupiter seemed to be considering Ted's story. "If you thought we stole it, why not just accuse us?"

"As I said, Jupiter, Mr. Harris thought you might perhaps have found it quite innocently. He pointed out that unfounded accusations are very dangerous."

"If you thought we had accidentally found it, why not just ask for it back?"

"Well, we discussed that, but Mr. Harris thought you might not want to admit that you'd picked it up. He thought you might be afraid to come forward."

"So you decided to contact us," Jupiter mused, "offer a reward, and let us think that you didn't know we had the amulet? You wanted to give us a way out, plus an incentive."

Ted nodded. "I'm really sorry, chaps, but I didn't know you then. Now that I know you, I know you'll give it back. You did find it, didn't you?"

"Bob and Pete did," Jupiter admitted, "but we can't give it back. We don't have it now." And Jupiter explained how the dark man had stolen the amulet from them.

"Then it's gone," Ted said, crestfallen.

Jupiter shook his head slowly. "No, there may still be a chance of recovering it. If we can find that man."

Ted grinned. "I say, some secret method? Can I help? I'd really like to work with you chaps."

"Maybe you can help, Ted," Jupiter agreed. "You keep your eyes open out here, and when we find the man we'll call you."

"Wonderful!" Ted beamed.

"But now we better get home," Jupiter said. "It's late."

Ted let them out through the gates. On their bikes they steered slowly toward the pass in the dark night. Pete was still puzzled as he rode beside the stocky First Investigator:

"Jupe, why didn't you tell what else Bob and I saw last night? About the call for help, and the laughing shadow?"

"Because I'm not sure Ted told us the truth," Jupiter

said grimly. "If he really thought we'd stolen that amulet, Pete, I think he would have denounced us right away—unless, for some reason, he doesn't want anyone else to know how we got the amulet. I think he's hiding something, Pete!"

Pete looked troubled as they began the long descent down from the pass to Rocky Beach.

"WHERE NO MAN CAN FIND IT!"

Early the next morning Bob jumped out of bed and dressed quickly. On his way downstairs he knocked on his parents' door.

"I'll get my own breakfast, Mom!"

Her sleepy voice answered, "All right, Bob. Clean up after yourself. Where will you be today?"

"At the salvage yard, Mom!"

In the sunny breakfast nook he ate a quick bowl of cereal, drank a glass of orange juice, and then called Pete. Pete's mother told him that Pete had already gone to the salvage yard. Bob washed his bowl and glass and ran for his bike.

At the salvage yard he ran full tilt into Aunt Mathilda.

"Well, at least I've found one of you! When you find the others, Bob, you tell Jupiter we'll need him to go with us to the Sandow Estate this morning."

"Yes, ma'am."

Bob walked casually to the rear of the salvage yard and, when Aunt Mathilda could no longer see him, hurried to the main entrance to the hidden trailer, and crawled into headquarters. As he came up through the trap door, he found Jupiter and Pete staring glumly at the silent telephone.

"No calls at all!" Pete announced in dejection. "Jupe's message recorder was blank."

Pete referred to the recording device Jupiter had built to attach to the telephone to record messages that came in while all three boys were out of headquarters.

"I'm afraid the Ghost-to-Ghost Hookup isn't working this time," Jupiter admitted.

"It may be too soon, Jupe," Bob said optimistically. "Listen to what I found out last night!"

"You listen to what we *saw!*" Pete countered, and told Bob about their adventure at the estate. Bob's eyes widened as he heard about Ted, the weird shapes, and the laughing shadow.

"Of course," Jupiter said, "they weren't headless midgets, but they sure looked like it. I was hoping there would be a message on the Ghost-to-Ghost this morning. I think that the dark men are the key to all the mystery, somehow, if we knew who they were and what they wanted. Bob, what did you find out about the Chumash Hoard?"

"It sure looks as if there's something to it according to the local history books," Bob reported. "After that renegade band disappeared, everyone started looking for the Hoard. They searched for a long time, but no one ever found it. One of the troubles was that the Chumash band had hideouts all over the mountains. The Sandow Estate was just one place where they hid. And no one ever found any clues to the where-abouts of the Hoard."

"Not even the two amulets Miss Sandow's brother had?" Pete asked. "Did the histories mention him?"

"Yes," Bob answered. "His name was Mark, and he killed a man and had to run away. It seemed to be sort of mysterious about the man he killed. He was a hunter who lived back in the hills on the estate. No one knew why Mark Sandow killed him. The records don't mention the two Chumash amulets."

"Professor Meeker said he'd never heard of the amulets," Jupiter said, frowning. "Did you find any reports on exactly what old Magnus Verde said be-fore he died?"

"In four different books," Bob reported, "and they were all different!" Bob dug out his notebook. "Ac-cording to one book Magnus Verde is supposed to have said, 'What man can find the eye of the sky?' Another writer quotes him as saying, 'The sky's eye finds no man.' And two others report that he said, 'It is in the eye of the sky where no man can find it.' I guess it wasn't easy to translate from Chumash."

"Professor Meeker explained that," Jupiter reminded him. "Besides, they're all pretty similar. Each one refers to the 'eye of the sky,' which the professor didn't mention, and they all say that Magnus Verde was sure no one could find the Hoard."

"But, Jupe," Pete said, "what does 'eye of the sky' mean?"

Jupiter thought. "Well, what is in the sky that looks sort of like an eye?"

"Some clouds sometimes?" Pete suggested.

"I know," Bob said, "the sun."

Jupiter nodded. "Or the moon. It's supposed to look like a face."

"How could they hide the Hoard in the moon, or the sun?" Pete objected.

"Not in the moon or sun, Pete," said Jupiter, "but maybe a place where the sun or moon always shines on some exact spot! The way the sun shone on certain temples in the old days."

"Sure," Bob said. "People used to build temples with a hole in the roof so that the sun would shine right on the altar."

"Only," the First Investigator went on unhappily, "this would have to be a very special place at a very special time."

Pete understood why Jupiter was unhappy. "You

mean we'd have to find the right spot at exactly the right moment in order to know that the sun or the moon ever does something special like that."

"I'm afraid so, Pete." Jupiter sounded dejected. Then he suddenly brightened. "Unless Magnus Verde didn't mean anything that complicated. For instance, he might have meant that the sun or moon *looks* like an eye through a certain mountain pass or valley. Do we know any place like that near here?"

"Gosh, Jupe, not that I ever heard of," Pete said. "Anyway, what if it isn't around here? Bob said that the Chumash band had hideouts all over."

"And Magnus Verde said no one could find it," Bob added.

"I'm convinced that Magnus Verde was taunting his captors with a riddle of some kind," Jupiter insisted. "If only we knew why that dark man wanted the statuette so much."

"Gosh, I forgot," Bob cried. "I've got more to tell you. That man and his friend attacked Mr. Harris!"

Bob repeated the news report that his Dad had heard on the radio the previous evening.

Jupiter jumped up.

"We should go and talk to Mr. Harris," the First Investigator said. "He could have learned something important. But one of us ought to stay with the phone. The recorder can't ask questions."

"It's Pete's turn," said Bob.

"I guess it is," Pete agreed.

"We'll take the walkie-talkies so Pete can contact us if he hears anything on the Ghost-to-Ghost," Jupiter said.

After finding the address of the Vegetarian League, Bob and Jupiter rode over on their bikes. It took only about ten minutes to reach the large Gothic house on Las Palmas Street that turned out to be Vegetarian League headquarters. It was the last house on the block, located right on the edge of town. The dry brown mountains came straight down to the road on the other side. There was an alley behind the houses on Las Palmas Street, where the residents had their garages.

The two boys parked their bikes at the gate, went up to the front door, and rang the bell. A short, heavy man opened the door. They asked for Mr. Harris.

"Boys!" called Mr. Harris himself from just behind the stocky man. "It's all right, Sanders, I know the boys. Come in! This is a pleasure. I hardly expected you here so soon. Have you come to join our League?"

The short man, Sanders, who was obviously an employee of Mr. Harris', went back to work on a pile of boxes in the dim entrance hall. Jupiter hastily explained that they had not come to become vegetarians.

"Er, no sir, we didn't come to join. We want to talk to you."

"Talk? Well, let's go into my office. Watch your step, we've hardly settled in here yet. I do wish you were here to join us. We need all the help we can get. Everything has to be done by myself, and my two most devoted assistants."

The boys picked their way through the jumble of boxes, books, filing cabinets and stacks of pamphlets. Mr. Harris ushered them through a heavy oak door and into a large, sunny room set up as an office. As he sat down behind an ancient desk, he waved the boys to chairs.

"Now, what's on your minds?"

Jupiter explained, "We heard about the attack on you, sir."

"Ah, yes, the crazy chap simply leaped on me. There were two of them, but only one actually attacked me. I was on the platform giving a brief talk. I defended myself, of course, and the audience began calling for the police, so the two men ran off."

"Why did they attack you, sir?" Bob asked.

"I simply don't know."

"Did they say anything?" Jupiter queried.

"Not in English. The rascal shouted a great deal, but it was all gibberish to me. I tried to capture him, but he eluded me. Both men were gone before the police arrived. I assume they were some fanatics who hate vegetarians. We've had to face that kind of ignorant prejudice many times. People often hate someone just because he is different from them, I'm afraid."

"I know that, sir," Jupiter said, "but I don't think those men were against you because you were a vegetarian."

Mr. Harris looked startled. "No? Then why *did* they attack me? Do you mean that you have some theory about it?"

"We sure do!" Bob said firmly. "We know . . ."

Bob stopped, suddenly aware of a faint sound somewhere in the office. Mr. Harris heard it, too, and began to look around with a puzzled frown. It was a very low *beep-beep-beep*. All at once Bob realized what it was. Pete must be trying to reach them on the walkie-talkies they were carrying.

Jupiter had heard it, too. He stood up abruptly. "I'm sorry, sir, but we have to go. We'll be back as soon as we can."

"Of course, Jupiter," Mr. Harris said. "I'll be here for a little while before I go to see Miss Sandow. I visit the dear lady every day. After all, without her I wouldn't have been able to start our league here in Rocky Beach."

"Yes, sir," Jupiter said, as he turned and hurried out of the office.

The boys knew that Pete could not reach them on their walkie-talkies while they were inside a building—at least not from such a distance. They walked rapidly through the haphazard stacks in the entry hall, and out into the sun of the open front yard. Jupiter found a large bush between the door and the gate,

and the two of them crouched down.

Jupiter pressed his sending button. "First here. Come in, Second. Come in, Second. We are receiving. Over."

Pete's voice came faintly from the small walkie-talkies. Jupe and Bob leaned close. "Second here. Do you read me? Come in, First! Do you read me? Over."

"First and Records receiving. Come in. Over." Jupiter spoke into his transmitter.

"Jupe?" Pete's faint voice sounded excited. "A report just came in on the Ghost-to-Ghost. A kid saw the dark men! They're in their car parked on Las Palmas Street near . . ."

Bob shouted, "Jupe! It's them! There they are!"

Jupiter jumped up. His fingers came off the receive button, cutting off Pete's voice, but neither Bob nor Jupiter was thinking about Pete. One of the dark men in the strange white clothes stood beside their bikes at the gate. The other was standing between them and the door of the house.

Both men began to move menacingly toward them, brandishing ugly knives. The boys could not reach their bikes. And they were also cut off from the house.

"Run!" Jupiter cried. "To the hills, Bob!"

PURSUIT IN THE HILLS

They turned and raced around the corner of the house. The two men stood there uncertainly for a moment, shouting. At the end of the yard, near the dry brown hills, the fence was low. The boys went over it without looking back.

"Up to the hills!" Jupiter panted.

They ran across the road and reached the first steep slope of the low mountains that ringed Rocky Beach. With Bob ahead, and Jupiter puffing behind him, they crashed their way up through the stiff, dry chaparral. The hard, thick, gray brush tore at their clothes. Behind them, they could hear the two dark men giving chase.

"What are they shouting?" Bob panted.

"I don't know," Jupiter cried. "I don't understand any of it! Just keep running!"

"Can we outrun them?"

"I . . . hope . . . so."

At the top of the first steep slope, they reached an old dirt road. They had gained on their pursuers. Out of sight for a moment, they turned and ran along the dirt road. They were running away from Rocky Beach, the Vegetarian League house, and their bikes, but there was no other way they could go. So they pounded along the dirt road looking for a way to escape.

"Oh, no!" Bob suddenly exclaimed.

The dirt road ended in a deep ravine. There had once been a bridge, but it was gone, and the steep sides were much too dangerous to climb down. The boys stopped in dismay.

"The bridge washed out in a flood!" Bob cried.

"Up the hill!" Jupiter pointed.

They began to climb up the slope of the mountain that towered hot and dusty above Rocky Beach. Below, they heard shouts. The two men had seen them and were pointing upward. While the boys were still looking back, their pursuers began to climb the slope with amazing speed and skill.

"They're gaining, Jupe!" Bob said.

"Keep climbing!"

They climbed and crawled upward in the blazing sun on the scorching slope. Their hands were bleeding from the sharp, iron-hard chaparral. At last they reached a high shoulder of the mountain. Jupiter dropped, panting, to the dirt. Bob looked back down.

"They're still coming!"

Jupiter groaned weakly. "Let them come. I'm dying."

Bob shaded his eyes. "We're faster runners, but they can climb better. They climb like goats. Hey, maybe they're two of those Yaquali! The Devils of the Cliffs."

Jupiter struggled up, revived by the prospect of seeing two Yaquali. "Maybe they're speaking Yaquali. No wonder we can't understand them."

"I don't care if they're speaking Eskimo," Bob declared. "How do we get away? Do you suppose Mr. Harris saw them chasing us."

"I doubt it," Jupiter said, peering across the distance. "Everything is quiet around the house."

"If we could only get back to our bikes!"

"We can't. They've cut us off. We'll just have to keep running."

"Where?" Bob said in despair, looking around the barren, scorched shoulder of the mountain. Then his eyes lighted up. "Jupe, come on! I know where we are now. I think there's a way to get away."

Bob started running along the shoulder that curved around the mountain. Jupiter puffed along behind; once more they were momentarily out of sight of their pursuers. Some fifty yards away around the corner of the mountain, Bob ran straight for a thick, dense growth of twisted live oaks and the impenetrable chaparral.

"Where are we running?" Jupiter was panting.

"Right there," Bob said.

Jupiter stared as Bob ran straight at the wall of dusty green trees and chaparral. "Where? I don't see . . ."

Bob vanished into the heavy brush before Jupiter could finish his question. The First Investigator plunged after the smaller boy—and suddenly found himself running in empty space!

He fell and landed with a thump at the bottom of a narrow gully totally hidden on all sides by the trees and the chaparral. Panting and bruised, Jupiter sat up, brushed himself off gingerly, and glared at his chum.

"You could have warned me," he complained.

"There wasn't time. I fell into this gully once when I was chasing a bull snake. They won't find us in here."

"Maybe," said Jupiter, unconvinced.

"Shhhhhhhh!" Bob hissed.

The boys crouched down in the gully and crawled silently to the bank. Bob peered through a thin gap in the brush. The two pursuers were standing not fifty feet away! They were talking, pointing all around, and arguing. Jupiter slumped down to the bottom of the gully.

"They know we're around here somewhere!"

"What do we do?"

"We keep quiet," the First Investigator pronounced.

They lay silent, listening. The two pursuers were walking and talking somewhere out beyond the dense brush. The boys could hear clearly, but they had no idea what the two dark men were saying—except that it sounded harsh and menacing.

Helpless, the boys could do nothing but wait. The voices came closer. There was the rustle and crash of bushes being searched.

Jupiter whispered, "I'm afraid it's only a matter of time until they find us. They seem to know that we didn't run beyond this point."

"This gully is pretty well hidden. They might miss it."

"Or they might stumble right into it. Is there any way we can get out of here unseen?"

Bob thought a moment. "There's a big ravine to the left that leads right back down to the road near the Vegetarian League house. Only we'd have to cross about fifty feet of open space from the end of this gully to get there."

"Fifty feet of open space?" Jupiter's brow was furrowed with concentration. "Then we have to have a diversion. Something to distract those men from seeing us cross that open space. If we could just get them down in here while we run for that ravine."

"If we were ventriloquists," Bob suggested, "we could throw our voices back here. Then, while they were coming down here after us, we could get to the ravine."

"Bob, that's it!" Jupiter seemed excited.

"What do you mean that's it? We're not ventriloquists. We can't throw our voices anywhere."

"Yes we can! By electronics." Jupiter picked up his walkie-talkie. "We'll leave one walkie-talkie here, turned up full volume, with the receive button held down. Then we'll go down to the end of the gully closest to that ravine, and———"

"And talk into the walkie-talkie so they'll hear us and think we're down here!"

"Exactly," Jupiter said. "They'll hear us, come to get us, and while they're out of sight down here we'll run to the ravine. By the time they find the walkie-talkie, they won't know where to look for us."

Quickly, Jupiter laid his walkie-talkie behind a bush at the bottom of the gully and placed a stone on the receive button. He picked up Bob's walkie-talkie, and the two boys crawled silently along the bottom of the gully until Bob nodded that they were as far as they could go.

"You see that big tree across the open space?" Bob whispered. "That's where the ravine is."

"Here goes," Jupiter whispered back. He squatted down and spoke into the walkie-talkie. "Bob! I hear them coming!"

Bob spoke into the speaker. "They won't find us down here! We're safe!"

Jupiter listened and heard Bob's voice, faint but clear, farther back in the gully where they had been hiding. He spoke once more into the walkie-talkie, while Bob peered through the brush to see what was happening.

"They hear it," Bob whispered. "They're going into the bushes."

"Now, Bob!" Jupiter hissed.

They jumped from the gully and ran full speed toward the big tree and the ravine. When they reached the tree, they looked back. The two dark men were nowhere in sight. The boys plunged down into the ravine and scrambled along the bottom toward the road far below.

Breathing hard, they came out into the street a half-block from the Vegetarian League house. The two men were still nowhere in sight.

"We better tell Mr. Harris that the dark men are back," said Jupiter.

They hastened around the corner to the front door. Jupiter rang the bell. They waited, but there was no answer. Bob began knocking. There was still no sound inside the house. He tried the door, but it was locked. Meanwhile Jupiter was peeking in at the window beside the door.

"He must have gone out to the estate," Bob said.

"I guess so," Jupiter agreed. "We better get out of here—fast!"

Without any further discussion they ran to their bicycles and pedaled away at top speed. They didn't slow down until they were back at the salvage yard.

JUPITER HAS A SUSPICION

Aunt Mathilda spied Bob and Jupiter the moment they rode into the salvage yard.

"There you are! . . . Jupiter Jones, are you ready to go to the Sandow Estate?"

"Yes, Aunt Mathilda," Jupiter said, "but we want to get something from my workshop first."

"You make it short, young man. Konrad and your uncle will be ready to go in two minutes."

The boys hurried to the workshop and through Tunnel Two into the hidden headquarters trailer. Pete was still at his post beside the telephone. He started talking at once.

"Why did you break off? I was trying to tell you

something important. Two kids called in. They spotted the dark men's car over on Las Palmas Street, and later they called back to report that the men were chasing two boys!"

"We know," Bob said ruefully.

"They were chasing us," Jupiter added. He explained how the dark men had appeared just as Pete was trying to talk to them, and described the chase in the hills.

"Wow!" Pete exclaimed. "You were sure lucky."

"Jupe was just too smart for them," Bob said.

But Jupiter was not waiting for compliments, he was too busy planning. "If those men are still hanging around the Vegetarian League house, they must want something. I think they might attack Mr. Harris again. If he's out with Miss Sandow, I'll see him when I go out there with Uncle Titus, and I can tell him what happened to Bob and me. But in case he should go back to the League before I see him, I think you fellows ought to go over to the house and wait for him."

"Gosh, First, I have to get home for lunch," Pete said.

"Me, too," Bob agreed.

"All right, but get over there again as soon as you can. Maybe you can spot those two men and keep an eye on them."

"But, Jupe, we just got away from them!" Bob protested.

Jupiter wasn't bothered by that fact. "I'm convinced

that that pair are after something important. I think they can lead us to the Chumash Hoard. Just be careful, and don't let them see you.

"That you don't have to tell us," Pete said.

"Do you think they're Yaquali, First?" Bob asked.

Jupiter nodded. "They must be, Pete. Somehow they must have learned about the Chumash Hoard, maybe through some old Indian writings or legends. It's possible that they understand old Magnus Verde's message."

"I wish *we* did." Pete sighed.

"So do I," Jupiter admitted. "It must be the clue to where the Hoard is—'in the eye of the sky where no one can find it.' We've got to puzzle it out."

"But, Jupe, if they've figured out what Magnus Verde was saying, what are they still looking for?"

"I just don't know," Jupiter said, biting his lip.

At that moment they all heard the distant voice of Aunt Mathilda:

"Jupiter Jones! Now where are you?"

"Don't forget, go and warn Mr. Harris, and see if you can find those dark men. But don't let them see you." Jupiter gave them their instructions once more. "And let's all think about that message of Magnus Verde's."

Bob and Pete nodded, and Jupiter hurried from the hidden headquarters. Out in the salvage yard the First Investigator found Konrad and Uncle Titus already in the big truck. His Aunt Mathilda was loading in a lunch hamper. Jupiter jumped into the cab, and Uncle Titus quickly told Konrad to drive off. Jupiter's uncle, a small man with an enormous mustache, was a most unusual junkman. He bought anything that interested him, not just because he thought he could sell it but because he liked it.

Soon the truck was out of Rocky Beach and driving up the steep and winding road into the pass. They reached the top of the pass and drove on to the iron gates of the Sandow Estate. The gates were open. Konrad roared through and pulled to a stop before the barn.

Uncle Titus jumped out as eagerly as Jupiter, excited as he always was when he was about to buy junk for the salvage yard. As they headed for the barn door, Miss Sandow came from the big house.

"You must be Titus Jones," the birdlike lady said. "I'm pleased to meet you. I hope you find many things you want. I've been accumulating this junk for far too long."

"I'm sure I will, ma'am," Uncle Titus said with a courtly bow and a flourish of his fine mustache. "You're sure you want to part with all of it?"

"Oh, dear me, yes! I think it's best to get it all cleared out. Since my nephew, Theodore, arrived I seem to have more interest in the estate. I want to get everything in order again."

"Then, with your assistance, Miss Sandow, I'll go in and select what I want to buy," Uncle Titus said.

Miss Sandow nodded, smiling, and accompanied Uncle Titus and Konrad into the barn. Jupiter lagged behind until he saw them vanish inside. Then he slipped away toward the big house to find Mr. Harris. Ted appeared behind him:

"Are you investigating something, Jupiter?" the English boy said eagerly.

"In a way, Ted," Jupiter admitted. "I want to talk to Mr. Harris."

"He's in the library."

Jupiter followed Ted into the house. They found Mr. Harris reading the Rocky Beach newspaper in the library. When the vegetarian saw Jupiter, he jumped up and hurried toward the First Investigator.

"Ted has reported his encounter with you boys last night." Mr. Harris announced at once. "I must apologize for my part in our little deception, and for thinking that you boys might be thieves. Because we suspected that you had the statuette, we thought it would be a good ruse to offer a reward for its return."

"I understand, sir," Jupiter said quietly.

"Good. Now tell me exactly what happened to the statuette."

Jupiter told Mr. Harris about the call for help that Bob and Pete had heard outside the estate wall, and the way the statuette had come flying over the wall. Mr. Harris listened intently, frowning from time to time. When Jupiter reached the part about the laughing shadow, Ted exclaimed:

"A shadow that laughed insanely? That's strange. I thought I heard a peculiar laugh myself last night."

"You're quite sure, Jupiter?" Mr. Harris asked. "It wasn't some trick of the wind, or the boys' imagination?"

"No, sir, there is a laughing shadow somewhere on this estate," the First Investigator insisted firmly. "And I think that whoever the shadow is he's holding some prisoners here."

"Really, Jupiter?" Ted said. "Prisoners? I say!"

"But why, Jupiter?" Mr. Harris said. "What is it all about?"

"The Chumash Hoard, sir. I'm sure of it."

"The what?" Mr. Harris said, incredulous.

"A vast hoard of gold," Jupiter said, and explained all that the boys had learned about the Chumash Hoard. Mr. Harris and Ted listened open-mouthed. When Jupiter had finished, Mr. Harris smiled.

"I see," he said. "I'm not sure I can believe such a legend—dying words and all—but I'll accept your contention that there may be some nefarious gang that does believe it. That could be quite dangerous. I'm not at all sure I like you boys being involved in such an affair."

"Would you repeat what that old Indian said, Jupiter?" Ted asked.

"Well, in essence," Jupiter explained, "he said that the Hoard was 'In the eye of the sky where no man could find it.' "

"Gosh, what could it mean?" Ted wondered. "And what does it have to do with Aunt Sarah's statuette? Why did you say that prisoners are being held on the estate?"

Before Jupiter could answer, they heard Miss Sandow calling from outside.

"Theodore! I need you for a moment. Where are you, Theodore?"

Ted hurried out of the house in answer to his aunt's summons. As soon as he had gone, Jupiter spoke quickly to Mr. Harris:

"Sir, I know the laughing shadow is real because I've heard it myself! And I know there are prisoners on the estate, because there was a message inside the amulet when we found it!"

"A message? Inside the statuette?" Mr. Harris looked concerned.

"A call for help," Jupiter said.

"Have you notified the police?"

"No, sir, we didn't really have anything to tell."

"No, I see that." Mr. Harris seemed to be considering the problem. "When did you see this laughing shadow?"

"Last night just before we met Ted," Jupiter said, and told Mr. Harris what he and Pete had seen at the lodge on the estate.

"What do you make of it, Jupiter?"

"I think that those four strange shapes were prisoners with bags over their heads! That's why it looked like they had no heads at all."

"What?" Mr. Harris exclaimed. "Four prisoners in our lodge? Held by that laughing shadow! Outrageous. How could such things go on right under Miss Sandow's nose?"

"How much do you really know about Ted Sandow, sir?" Jupiter said bluntly.

"Ted?" Mr. Harris gaped, blinked. "You think that Ted is involved? By thunder, I'm going to get to the bottom of this! Come on, Jupiter, I want to look at that lodge!"

Mr. Harris strode to the desk and opened a drawer. When he turned, he held a pistol in his hand.

CALL THE POLICE!

Mr. Harris gripped the pistol grimly as he and Jupiter moved silently along the forest path toward the lodge. The vegetarian's ruddy face was serious and determined as they hastened on under the shadows of the trees.

"And you think that the dark men who attacked you and took the statuette are the same ones who attacked me?" Mr. Harris said as he walked.

"They must be, sir."

"If that's true, they may also be the ones who are holding prisoners out here. We had better approach the lodge with caution."

"They'll probably be gone by now, sir, especially if the shadow saw Bob and me last night."

"That remains to be seen. If they're so bold as to hold prisoners right on the estate, they may not have been scared by two boys. What I don't understand is what they think they're up to, you see."

"I guess I don't understand that, either," Jupiter admitted unhappily. "Maybe the prisoners are the ones who really know the secret of where the Hoard is, and those dark men and the laughing shadow are trying to find it."

"That could be, Jupiter. Yes, you may have hit on it. And perhaps we can catch the ruffians red-handed!"

They hurried on as quietly as they could in the deep forest shadows and came to where the smaller path led down into the bowl-shaped valley. The truck no longer stood in front of the lodge. The building looked much less mysterious in the bright noon sunlight.

Mr. Harris motioned for Jupiter to crouch low in the trees and be silent. Then he began to work his way stealthily down the slope through the trees. Jupiter examined the lodge closely. There was no sign of movement anywhere. The shutters on the lodge windows were open, and so was the front door. As soon as he saw the open door Jupiter was certain that there would be no one inside.

Mr. Harris wasn't taking any chances. He continued to slip silently down through the trees until he reached the edge of the open clearing at the bottom of the valley. There he stopped for a moment, surveying the lodge. On the rim of the valley, Jupiter fidgeted under the enforced inaction. But then Mr. Harris left the trees and ran to a corner of the lodge, holding his pistol in one hand. Jupiter watched him peer in at a window.

Mr. Harris left the window and ran around to the open front door. He went inside quickly. Jupiter waited. He could hear a lot of noise inside the lodge. Then Mr. Harris appeared at the door and waved. Jupiter scrambled down the path and joined the vegetarian in front of the lodge.

"Empty, lad. I looked under everything. Not a hair of them, but they were here all right. Look."

Mr. Harris displayed a pair of small white trousers of a homespun material exactly like that worn by the two dark men.

"I should guess that it was Indian clothing, right enough. It looks as if your dark men were here. And the truck you saw was really here, too. There's an oil patch on the roadway. Dry, though. I'd say the truck has been gone for some time."

"Is there any sign of where they might have gone, Mr. Harris?" Jupiter asked.

"None that I could find, but let's take another look. Maybe you can spot something."

They went inside the lodge. Jupiter surveyed the scene. It was clear that the men he had seen last night had left the lodge in a hurry. Empty bottles lay around on the tables; remains of a meal had dried and hardened on unwashed plates still on the tables. But Jupiter could find nothing that gave even a hint as to where the men had gone.

"I guess there's nothing here," he said, at last. "But I'm sure they must be somewhere on the estate!"

Mr. Harris shook his head. "It's an awfully large estate, Jupiter. And most of it is mountainous. I'm afraid the rascals are gone. I'm sure that when you spotted them you blew their entire scheme and they ran."

"I don't think so, sir," Jupiter insisted. "I think they're still trying to find something. They chased Bob and me when we left your office."

"Chased you? At *my* house?" Mr. Harris stared at Jupiter in astonishment. "But what could they want from you now?"

"Not from us, Mr. Harris. From you!" Jupiter declared.

"From me? What on earth could they want from me?"

"There must be something, sir. After they stole our amulet, they attacked you during your lecture. Then when we left your office today they chased us again. They must have thought that you had given something to us."

"Well, I'm . . . By Jove!" Mr. Harris cried. "The other statuette! I took it to my office for safe keeping the very night the first one was stolen. I insisted Miss Sandow entrust it to me. I had completely forgotten about it. They must want both amulets."

Jupiter nodded eagerly. "They probably need both of them to tell them where the hoard is."

"Yes, that's probably it," Mr. Harris agreed. "What I don't understand is how those men could have known I had the second amulet at my office."

"They must have seen you take it there."

"Impossible. It was in a box, and I carried it in my pocket. They couldn't have spied on me in my office, either."

"Could one of your assistants have told them?" Jupiter asked.

"No, they're old friends and staunch vegetarians. Anyway, they knew nothing about the amulet."

Jupiter chewed at his lower lip, a sure sign that he was concentrating. "Well, sir, Miss Sandow herself must have known you had it. So that's one person."

"I hardly think that Sarah Sandow is in cahoots with the thieves. Even if she wanted to look for the Hoard, she already had the amulets. And Sarah and Ted are the only——"

Jupiter interrupted, "Ted? . . . *He* knew?"

Mr. Harris stood with his mouth open, then slowly closed it again. "This could be very serious, Jupiter. Poor Miss Sandow—if Ted is involved in some devious scheme—it could break her heart."

"He was at the gate after Bob and Pete found the first amulet," Jupiter pointed out, "and he was out in the dark last night. How well do you know him, Mr. Harris?"

"Not well at all, actually. We met in England just as he was coming here. I was on my way to Los Angeles, so when he told me his aunt was a vegetarian, I decided to come to see her and try to enlist her support." Mr. Harris stopped again. He looked grim. "We'd better talk to young Ted—right away!"

Jupiter had to trot to keep up with Mr. Harris as they hurried from the lodge and back through the forest to the house. Uncle Titus and Konrad were still loading the truck. As Mr. Harris strode into the house to find Ted, Uncle Titus saw Jupiter.

"There you are! Did you come here to work or not, you young scalawag!" Uncle Titus roared.

Reluctantly, Jupiter began to help Konrad carry an ornate old wardrobe trunk to the truck. As he worked he glanced now and then at the door of the house. Time seemed to crawl, and Jupiter fumed with impatience as he worked. Then Mr. Harris reappeared.

"Ted drove off somewhere. I think I had better return to my office."

"If Ted goes to your office, he'll be seen," Jupiter said with a grin. "Bob and Pete are there watching right now."

Mr. Harris seemed to freeze. "What?"

"I sent them to watch for the dark men," Jupiter explained.

"Jupiter!" Mr. Harris cried, turning pale. "That second amulet is still there in my safe. If those boys attempt any foolish move they could be in great danger! I'll drive in at once. Your uncle is almost finished here. As soon as you get to Rocky Beach go to the police."

With that ominous instruction, Mr. Harris ran for his car and drove off at a breakneck pace down the private road to the highway.

CAUGHT!

After lunch, Bob and Pete met again at the salvage yard. They checked the telephone recorder but found no messages, so they left right away for the headquarters of the Vegetarian League.

They approached cautiously, alert for any signs of the dark men, but there was no sign of activity at the big Gothic house. Mr. Harris' car was not in front or in the alley behind, and the front door was locked.

"He must be out at the estate," Pete decided.

"Jupe'll talk to him then," Bob said, "but we better stay here. Maybe those men will come back."

There was a narrow alley between two silent houses across the street from the Vegetarian League headquarters. Bob and Pete decided to squat down there beside their bikes and wait for developments. The barren hills where the dark men had chased Bob and Jupiter were baking in the bright sun, and for a long time nothing moved in the heat. A single turkey vulture sailed high above the hills. Pete eyed the great, soaring black bird uneasily.

"I hope that buzzard isn't thinking of us," he said.

"Vultures are very important to nature," Bob protested. "They keep the wilderness clean and healthy. They're really harmless and necessary."

"They're not necessary to me," Pete declared. "I don't like to think about what that one has on its hungry mind."

For an hour not even a car passed on the hot street. Pete grew impatient and began to play with the small stones that lay in the alley. After a while he moved his legs, which were stiff from squatting so long, and groaned:

"This is one part of being an investigator I don't much like—waiting and watching."

"Jupe says it's the most important part," Bob declared. "Real investigators sometimes watch the same place for weeks."

"Not me, thank you," Pete said, and groaned again with impatience. "Why does First think those dark men'll come back here?"

"I think Jupe figures that they want something Mr. Harris has. Some other clue to the Hoard."

"Gosh, then they might show up any time." Pete

peered across the street with revived interest.

"Exactly, and that's why it's so important to watch."

Suddenly, from across the hot and sunny street, there came a muffled shout.

"Hello! Someone! Hello out there!"

The cry was faint but clear in the stillness of the hot afternoon.

"Hey, out there! Help!"

Pete whispered, "It's from the League house. In the back."

"Maybe Mr. Harris is locked in," Bob said. "Maybe the thieves attacked him again."

The boys hesitated. If the dark men were around, they might get into trouble if they showed themselves. But if Mr. Harris really was locked in, they ought to try to help him.

"What'll we do?" Pete asked.

"I guess we better take a look, but let's be careful, Pete. If we see anything of those men we better get away fast."

They crossed the empty street warily. Since they knew the front door was locked, they went cautiously around to the rear of the house and tried the back door.

"It's open," Pete whispered, as he turned the knob. He pushed the door open, and they walked along a dark hallway until they came to what had been the kitchen of the old house. It was empty now.

They went through a swinging door into the rear of the cluttered entry hall. In the dim, cool hall they listened.

"I don't hear anything," Bob whispered.

"But I know that call came from somewhere in here," Pete insisted. "Let's try the office."

They opened the office door carefully, but the room was silent and empty. Bob pointed to a closet door. The two boys tiptoed over to it and listened for a minute. There was no sound. Gingerly, Bob opened the door while Pete stood to one side, holding a heavy paperweight from Mr. Harris' desk.

The closet was empty.

"That shout had to come from somewhere," Pete said.

"Maybe he's shut in where there isn't enough air, and he's collapsed," Bob suggested.

"Gosh, that could be," Pete agreed. "We better hurry and look everywhere."

Quickly they searched all the rooms downstairs. Finding nothing, they went up to the second floor. There they looked into a large meeting room that had been made from three smaller rooms. It had a platform at one end. Obviously this was the place where Mr. Harris had been attacked during his lecture.

"Hello! Hello! I hear you! Help!" The cry came again, from overhead.

Bob exclaimed, "He must be on the third floor!"

"Come on!" Pete cried, already running for the stairs.

There was little light on the third floor. The windows were shuttered, and dust lay thick on a pile of planks strewn about the floor. The doors to all the rooms along the dark corridor were open. The boys stood there, listening intently.

Suddenly there was a frantic banging at the far end of the corridor. Pete picked up a large two-by-four, and together they walked down the hall. The room at the end of the corridor was bare and completely empty. They stood there for a moment, waiting for another shout or a bang. Then Bob noticed the door on the far side of the room.

"There, Pete!"

Pete nodded, and the two boys approached the closed door. Bob tried the knob, while Pete stood ready with his two-by-four.

"It's locked," Bob said. "Can we break it down?"

Behind them the door to the corridor slammed shut. They whirled, their eyes wide and startled. Pete held his two-by-four ready to repel any attack. But no one was there. Only the closed door.

"Pete!" Bob cried.

The lock on the room door clicked from outside, and a familiar voice roared with laughter beyond the locked door.

"Boy, are you smart guys ever dumb!" the laughing voice sneered. The voice of Skinny Norris!

Bob and Pete rushed to the door, but it was tightly locked. Although Pete tugged and pulled and raged, he couldn't budge it.

"Skinny Norris, you let us out of here!" Bob yelled.

"If you don't," Pete threatened, "we'll fix you when we get out of here. We'll——"

"But you won't get out." Skinny taunted them through the door. "I'm just going to let the two of you stew in there. Serve you nosy brats right. Too bad Fatso Jones isn't with you. I'd like to see that fat smart aleck trying to get out of there."

"You wouldn't talk like that if Jupiter was here," Bob said angrily.

"You shut up, Bob Andrews!" Skinny shouted. The envious Skinny hated to have anyone suggest that he wasn't a match for Jupiter. "You're in bad trouble, you hear?"

"You're the one who's going to be in trouble," Pete said. "What do you think you're doing anyhow?"

"What am I doing?" Skinny snickered out in the corridor. "Why, I'm protecting private property, that's what I'm doing! I heard noises in here when I was passing by. I came in, and guess what? I caught two trespassers cold."

"You're crazy, Skinny! No one'll believe you."

"No? The front door was locked and no one was here. Just what were you doing coming in the back way?" Skinny laughed nastily. "I've been watching that junk yard of Fatso's uncle ever since Ted Sandow asked about you. I knew I'd catch you at something."

Bob groaned. "Skinny, Mr. Harris knows we're here. We're working for Miss Sandow."

"Don't try to fool me," Skinny said from the corridor. "Ted Sandow told me he was looking for a valuable statuette, and I could tell he thought you three had stolen it."

"Oh, no!" Pete cried. "That was before we talked to Ted. He's the one who hired us to find the statuette. Why don't you stop trying to be smarter than Jupiter?"

"I *am* smarter than that fat show-off! You can just sweat it out in there. If Fatso Jones is so smart let him rescue you. I'm taking off. So long, wise guys!"

Bob looked despairingly at Pete, then walked over to the locked door. He could hear Skinny going downstairs. After a long time, they heard the back door slam.

Bob and Pete looked at each other hopelessly as Bob moved away from the door. They were obviously in a bad spot.

"The windows are barred," Pete said, "and that other door is locked solid."

"It's an old house," Bob suggested. "How about the walls or the floor? Maybe we can find a weak spot—a loose board or something."

Pete wasn't optimistic, but he inspected the floor while Bob studied the walls. Unfortunately there were no weak spots in the floor.

"The walls are solid as a rock, too," Bob said glumly.

"Maybe Jupiter or Mr. Harris will come soon," Pete suggested.

"Our bikes are still in that alley. Jupe'd see them."

"Sure," Pete agreed, "he'd know we were in here somewhere."

The boys grinned at each other, but the grins were feeble. Each was aware of the fact that he was trying to convince the other that Jupiter would somehow come to their rescue.

"Maybe," Bob said weakly, "Mr. Harris will come back."

"And maybe he won't, or not for a long time. Maybe he won't come back until tomorrow."

"There has to be some way out!" Bob insisted.

They looked all around the small room again without much real hope. They were stuck, and they knew it. Trapped by that stupid Skinny Norris.

"Bob!" Pete cried, staring at something behind his fellow investigator. "The door! It opens inward. The hinges are right there inside."

"We can push out the hinge pins!"

"Sure, it'll be easy. Boy, is that Skinny dumb."

"But we don't have any tools," Bob said.

"Oh, yes, we do." Pete pulled out his heavy scout knife with its many strong blades and quickly went to work. The hinge pins were covered with old paint, and were very stiff. Pete began to sweat as he struggled to loosen them.

Bob stood anxiously beside him, trying to help as much as he could.

Finally, the last hinge pin fell into Pete's hand. Bob grasped the upper hinge, and Pete grabbed the lower. They counted to three and pulled. The door swung inward, broke free of the lock, and fell to the floor with a loud crash.

They lunged through the doorway together and headed for the stairway. From down below came the unexpected sound of heavy footsteps.

Someone—or something—was coming up the stairs.

JUPITER HAS A HUNCH

At the Sandow Estate Jupiter had been working feverishly carrying the junk from the barn to the truck. The First Investigator was alarmed by Mr. Harris' worry over Bob and Pete. Although he was sure that Bob and Pete could take care of themselves, Mr. Harris might be right about their being in danger. Jupiter wanted to contact Chief Reynolds right away.

When the truck was finally loaded, Jupiter climbed into the cab and chewed on his lower lip as Miss Sandow came from the house to talk to Uncle Titus.

"Mr. Jones," the birdlike lady said, "I can't imagine what you'll do with all that ancient clutter of mine."

"Don't you worry, ma'am," Uncle Titus said gallantly, twirling his enormous mustache. "I'll sell it all at a handsome profit, I'm sure. Now you just see that you charge me properly."

"Goodness, I wish Ted were here. I haven't the slightest notion what to charge. Knowing your boys seems to have made Theodore so happy, I really feel I should give it to you. Especially if they can find my little statuette for me."

"Find your statuette?" Uncle Titus sounded puzzled. Jupiter held his breath, for Uncle Titus wasn't always pleased about the boys being investigators. But this time the peppery little man was too happy about his truckload of new junk to be displeased. He nodded. "Well, the boys do seem to have a knack for that sort of thing. Now, let's consider what I owe you, ma'am."

Jupiter almost bit a piece out of his lip in impatience, but at last Uncle Titus settled his business, and the truck rolled out of the estate in the direction of Rocky Beach. Konrad drove at his usual headlong pace and soon they reached the salvage yard. Jumping out of the truck, Jupiter rushed to the hidden trailer. Aunt Mathilda and Uncle Titus were far too excited by their purchases to notice his quick escape.

He crawled into Headquarters through the main tunnel, and emerged through the trapdoor in the floor. Bob and Pete were not there. Quickly, the

First Investigator activated the telephone-record-ing-machine. There were no messages at all. Wor-ried now, and remembering Mr. Harris' instruc-tions, Jupiter crawled back out and left the junk yard through Red Gate Rover.

He walked the few blocks from the salvage yard to Rocky Beach Police Headquarters. He asked at once for Chief Reynolds and, because the boys were well-known to the Rocky Beach police, he was soon sitting across a desk from the Chief himself.

"Well, what can I do for you, Deputy?" Chief Reynolds said with a smile. He was referring to the honorary junior deputy title given the boys for help on a previous case.

"We're working on a case, sir," Jupiter said quickly, "and I think we need to call you in now."

"All right, suppose you tell me all about it."

"There isn't time, sir! Mr. Harris . . ."

"Slow and steady, Jupiter," the Chief instructed. "Start at the beginning. That's the way to give a re-port."

"Yes, sir," Jupiter agreed reluctantly. He started to tell the Chief about the amulet and the laughing shadow the first night Bob and Pete had seen them. He talked rapidly in an effort to finish his story as fast as possible.

"Whoa!" Chief Reynolds stopped him. "A laugh-ing shadow? Bob and Pete must have been letting their imaginations run high, don't you think?"

"No, sir," Jupiter said. "Last night I heard it myself, and it was really spooky. It was tall, too, but I didn't think it looked humpbacked. Pete and Bob were closer, of course, and they said it had a small head and beaky nose that kept jerking around.

"While Pete and I were watching it, a truck drove up with four headless midgets!"

Chief Reynolds coughed. "Headless midgets?"

"Well, no, not really. I mean, sir, they *looked* like that, but I think they had bags over their heads. They were prisoners in that lodge, you see, and someone had put bags on their heads so that they couldn't see."

"And you think that it could have been one of those 'midget' prisoners who called for help and threw the amulet over the wall?"

"That's right, sir," Jupiter said. "I think one of those prisoners stole the amulet and then hid his message for help in it. When he was recaptured, he threw it over the wall in the hope that someone would find it."

"In a hidden compartment? Pretty slim chance, Jupiter."

"I'm sure he was desperate, Chief. Maybe he expected some friends to be around, but they weren't and we found it. Then the two dark men attacked us to get the amulet back. *They* probably wanted the amulet for itself. I doubt if they even knew about the message."

"Dark men?" Chief Reynolds snapped. "What dark men?"

"I'm sorry, sir, you're right about telling it in order. I forgot to mention them." The First Investigator described the two dark men who had pursued the boys and attacked Mr. Harris.

"Oh, *those* men!" the Chief sounded almost relieved. "Well, now they're easier to believe in than laughing shadows and headless midgets. We're looking for that pair ourselves after their attack on Harris. All right, Jupiter, let's go and see your Mr. Harris at once."

The Chief summoned two of his men, and with Jupiter they hastened out to the Chief's car. They drove straight to the old house of the Vegetarian League. As they turned into the deserted street on the edge of the town, Jupiter saw Mr. Harris' car parked in front of the house.

"He must be here," Jupiter said. "That's his car."

Mr. Harris opened the front door before they had a chance to knock. Looking straight at Jupiter, he asked anxiously, "Where are Bob and Pete? I was expecting to find them here."

"I don't know," Jupiter said. "I thought they'd be here, too. Did you find Ted anywhere?"

"No, I didn't. I thought I spotted his car near your salvage yard, but if it was Ted he got away from me. I came straight home." For the first time, Mr. Harris looked curiously at Chief Reynolds.

"Oh!" Jupiter suddenly remembered his manners. "This is Chief Reynolds, Mr. Harris. He's going to help us."

"It was good of you to come over, Chief," said Mr. Harris in his usual brisk manner. "We seem to have some problems here. When those intruders first broke up my meeting, I thought it was just an attack by some typical anti-vegetarians. They can be quite fanatical, you know. But from what Jupiter has told me, I'm beginning to understand that it may be much more serious than that."

"You mean the laughing shadow and those headless prisoners?" Chief Reynolds asked.

"Well, perhaps the boys are a bit overwrought about those matters. I understand they don't really agree on what the laughing shadow sounded like. But it does seem as if there is some plot afoot involving Miss Sandow's gold statuettes."

Chief Reynolds looked thoughtful. "The Chumash Hoard is a local legend, and it may well exist. From what I've heard, a lot of people might risk a great deal to get it."

"And *do* a great deal," Mr. Harris said grimly. But just now I'm not concerned with the Hoard. I'm worried about Bob and Pete. According to Jupiter, they should be here."

"We'd better have a look around," Chief Reynolds decided, "in case they were here before you returned."

Inside, Mr. Harris and Jupiter searched the first floor. Chief Reynolds and his men examined the upper floors. When they met again outside Mr. Harris' office, no one had found a trace of Bob and Pete. Jupiter was alarmed.

"They've got to be around here somewhere!" he declared.

Mr. Harris frowned. "You don't think that perhaps they saw the dark men and followed them?"

"That would be just like the boys," Chief Reynolds acknowledged.

"But they would have reported in, sir," Jupiter said.

"Perhaps not at once, Jupiter," Mr. Harris said.

"That's right," the Chief agreed. "They might not have had a chance yet. But I don't much like the idea of them trailing after those two men like that."

Jupiter was not convinced, but he had to admit that if Bob and Pete had spotted the two men they might well have tried to follow them and find out where they were hiding. It was what he himself would have done.

"I think we'd better start looking for the boys," Chief Reynolds decided.

"At once!" Mr. Harris agreed. "But before you go, Chief, I'd like you to take the second amulet to your office. I don't want to keep it here."

They went into Mr. Harris' office. The vegetarian strode to his safe, opened it, and took out a small

box. He carried the box to his desk, which was lit-
tered with the remains of a hurried meal.

"Pardon the mess, I was eating a snack at my
desk," he said, sweeping the debris into his wastebasket, and opening the box. "There, that's what all
the fuss seems to be about."

They crowded around and looked down at the
second grinning little gold man. The Chief examined
it, shaking his head in bafflement over what impor-
tance it could have, then passed it along to Jupiter.
The First Investigator opened the secret compartment, but found it was empty.

"No message in this one, sir," he said.

"Then it looks as if those two ruffians are after the
amulet itself, wouldn't you say?" Mr. Harris com-
mented. "I'll feel better with it in the hands of the
police. At least, no one can steal it, and we can turn
our attention to tracking down the villains and finding out what they're up to."

"Maybe Bob and Pete can tell us where to find
them," Chief Reynolds said. "That is, if we can just
locate Bob and Pete. Come on, Jupiter, I think
we'd better start looking for them."

"Call me the instant you have any information
and let me know if there is anything I can do," Mr.
Harris said. "Tomorrow I'm going to ask young Ted
Sandow some questions." Harris' voice sounded
stern. "I hope he has an explanation."

Outside on the street again, the Chief and his

men hurried to their car. Jupiter followed more slowly, his keen eyes searching the hot, sunny neighborhood. Suddenly, the stocky First Investigator pointed to the small alley between two old houses across the street.

"Chief! I see something! Tire marks over there!"

Jupiter raced across the street. Chief Reynolds caught up to him in the narrow alleyway.

"They were here, Chief! I recognize a patch in Bob's tire tracks. They must have been hiding in this alley, watching the house. Look, on the ground there!"

Where Pete had crouched, waiting, there was a small pile of stones in the shape of a crude cone.

"Pete always piles stones like that," Jupiter said. "It's a reflex."

"Then they must have seen someone and followed them. Their bikes aren't here."

Jupiter looked all around the alley. "I don't know, sir. They should have left some sign if they had done that. We always carry colored chalk to leave a trail."

"They probably didn't have time. We'll send out an All-Points-Bulletin on them at once. I don't think we ought to alarm their parents yet."

"No, sir," Jupiter agreed. "Possibly they're back at the salvage yard by now."

"I hope so, son," Chief Reynolds said. "I only wish we had more to go on. I'm sure we'll find the dark men eventually, but I wish I had a better idea of who that laughing shadow could be."

"He's tall, sir. We know that. And the two men are quite short. Ted Sandow is tall."

"But you boys are familiar with Ted Sandow's voice, right? Wouldn't you know if he was the laughing shadow?"

"We ought to." Jupiter frowned, obviously in deep concentration. "But that laugh certainly didn't sound like anyone *I* know."

"The way you describe it, it doesn't really sound like a voice at all."

"That's it!" Jupiter exclaimed. "No voice at all! At least not a human kind of voice. It reminds me of a story by Edgar Allan Poe, where no one understood the murderer's language because the murderer turned out to be an ape. Only this was no ape. But isn't there something . . . something in Australia, I think, that has a laugh that sounds——"

"What are you talking about, Jupiter?"

Jupiter chewed his lip in despair. "I . . . I can't remember exactly but I know it has something to do with an animal from Australia. Ted Sandow has an accent. He says he's from England, but maybe he isn't. Maybe he's an impostor from Australia."

"Well, if you're talking about accents, what about Harris himself?" Chief Reynolds asked. "He sounds like a Limey to me."

Jupiter's eyes brightened. "Chief!" he exclaimed. "Do you think Harris could be an Australian? I don't think that is a British accent at all."

"I don't know, but I'll contact the Australian authorities right away and ask about both of them. We can certainly provide a good description."

They drove back to police headquarters, where the Chief went to work immediately. He sent out the All-Points-Bulletin (APB) on Bob and Pete. It would alert the police in Rocky Beach and the whole county to be on the lookout for the boys. He also placed a call to Australia.

Jupiter hurried back to the salvage yard, but there was no one inside the hidden trailer. Scared now, he sat and stared at the telephone. What if Bob and Pete were prisoners? There might not be time for an APB to find them. He couldn't just sit there waiting. If he went back to Mr. Harris' house, he might still find some clue he hadn't noticed earlier.

He picked up the telephone to call the Rent-'n-Ride Auto Rental Company. If he found a sign from Bob and Pete, he might want to be able to move quickly.

A VILLAIN UNMASKED

Fifteen minutes later Jupiter slipped out through Green Gate One and ran to the waiting Rolls-Royce.

"The Vegetarian League, Worthington, and fast," the First Investigator said urgently, and gave the address.

"Instantly, Master Jones."

The magnificent gold-plated vehicle glided smoothly along the streets and turned into Las Palmas Street toward the Gothic headquarters of the Vegetarian League. Jupiter scanned the street anxiously for any signs of his chums.

When the Rolls-Royce was a block away, Mr. Harris' car came tearing down the street toward them and passed in a cloud of dust. Jupiter started to shout to him, but Mr. Harris didn't even glance at the Rolls-Royce. The vegetarian was bent grimly over his steering wheel, his face dark and brooding.

"Was that a gentleman you know, Master Jones?" Worthington asked. "Shall I attempt to catch him?"

"He said he was going to wait for news about Bob and Pete," Jupiter said, looking back at the vanishing car. "But maybe something happened to change his plans. Just drive on to the house, Worthington."

Worthington continued on, and the big car slid silently to a stop at the front door. Jupiter was out like a shot, with Worthington striding up the walk behind him. The front door was open. Jupiter raced inside and stood listening.

"Do you hear anything, Worthington?"

"No, Master Jones. What are we looking for?"

"Bob and Pete," the First Investigator replied. "Some sign from them, probably in chalk, or some clue that shows they were in here."

"You feel that they may be in some difficulty?"

"I don't know," Jupiter admitted. "The Chief thinks they're off somewhere on their own, and maybe he's right, but I'm sure they would have left some sign in that case."

"I agree," Worthington said quietly.

"Chief Reynolds and his men searched the upper floors, but they might not have noticed a chalked sign. You go and look upstairs, Worthington, and I'll look out in the street again."

"Very good, Master Jones."

Jupiter covered the whole street, examining walls and fences for chalk marks. He also looked on the ground for any marks or message scratched in the dirt, and he inspected the trees. He found nothing at all beyond that small conical pile of stones he was sure had been made by Pete.

Inside the house again, he met Worthington coming down from the upper floors. The tall chauffeur shook his head:

"Nothing that I could interpret as a sign, Master Jones."

Jupiter frowned. "Maybe the Chief and Mr. Harris are right. I guess I better go back to the salvage yard and wait for them. . . . I wonder where Mr. Harris was driving so fast?"

"Perhaps Chief Reynolds called him," Worthington suggested. "But may I point out, we have not examined this first floor."

"I did that the first time," Jupiter said glumly.

"Possibly you overlooked some small thing. A second look will not be amiss."

They went into Mr. Harris' office. Jupiter saw no marks on the walls, and Worthington discovered nothing on the floor or in the closet. Jupiter looked into Mr. Harris' desk and wastebasket. He had turned away from the desk when he stopped abruptly and went back to the wastebasket.

"Worthington!" he cried. "Look at this!"

The chauffeur hurried over, and took the piece of

wax paper from his hand. Worthington blinked in puzzlement.

"It's simply a sandwich wrapper, Master Jones. I fail to see the significance."

"Look at those stains on it! That brownish stain, and the red stain! See?" Jupiter pointed.

Worthington nodded. "Yes, I see them. Mustard and some blood, I should say. Not uncommon on a sandwich wrapper." The fastidious chauffeur gingerly touched the brown stain, and sniffed at it. "Mustard, definitely. Rather hot, too."

"But, Worthington, Mr. Harris is the president of the Vegetarian League!" Jupiter cried. "Don't you see? If he was eating a sandwich with meat and mustard in it, he must be a fraud!"

"By George, Master Jupiter. Are you certain this was Mr. Harris' sandwich?"

"He said so himself," Jupiter answered. "And if he's a fake vegetarian, I'll bet the whole League is a fake. Mr. Harris started the group here in Rocky Beach and he claimed he had a big organization somewhere else. But I'll bet he doesn't have any organization at all!"

"A serious charge, Master Jones," Worthington said severely, "What purpose could he have?"

"Don't you see?" said Jupiter. "He knew that Miss Sandow was a vegetarian. Ted told him so in England. I'll bet he managed to meet Ted on purpose. He probably knew about the Chumash Hoard and wanted to find it. He used Ted and his fake Vege-tarian League to get close to Miss Sandow. It was a good way to gain entry to the Sandow Estate."

"You mean he knew about the Hoard before he ever came here, or met young Ted?"

"I wouldn't be at all surprised. He probably tried to make us suspicious of Ted on purpose." Jupiter groaned. "And to think I told him all about what we had guessed. I actually warned him."

"You had no way of knowing, Master Jones," Worthington said. "Apparently he has fooled every-one."

"He sure has. Why, he may even be the laughing shadow. Maybe he's holding those four headless prisoners himself." Suddenly Jupiter's eyes widened in dismay. "Worthington! We have to get to Chief Reynolds at once."

"Of course, Master Jones. You've thought of a plan to foil his scheme?"

"No," Jupiter said, "but I've just realized that Mr. Harris played a trick on us. He was very late getting here from the estate, and he said it was because he thought he saw Ted near the salvage yard, but that was a lie! He must have been here long before us—and he must have seized Bob and Pete!"

THE DARK MEN APPEAR

Mr. Harris sat on the rustic table in the center of the unpainted room, looking thoughtfully at Bob and Pete.

"This truly hurts me, boys, you see," he said.

Bob and Pete did not answer. They were seated against a board wall, their hands and feet tied securely. They had little idea where they were, only that they had been brought to some small cabin in the mountains after their capture in the Vegetarian League house by Harris.

They realized now that Mr. Harris must be connected with the laughing shadow. But there was nothing they could do, and no one they could tell. Mr. Harris and his two assistants had pounced on them, in the corridor of the house, hustled them out to a truck, and tied them. Then the two assistants had

driven them off with their bicycles. Mr. Harris himself had apparently remained at the League house
for a while, because this was his first appearance at
the cabin.

He smiled sadly at them. "Unfortunately, you boys
do have a way of appearing where you're not wanted,
eh? Snooping around my house, for instance. I'm
sure you found nothing, but it pays to be safe, you
know? Fortunately I had time to remove all traces
of your presence before the police arrived.

"I'm afraid I shall have to keep you as my guests
for a time. Until, shall we say, I am far from this
location. Luckily, my work here is almost finished
now."

Bob burst out for the first time, "You're a thief!"

"You're trying to steal the Chumash Hoard," Pete
cried hotly.

Mr. Harris laughed aloud. "Yes, you are clever
boys. The Chumash Hoard is precisely what I'm after,
and I shall steal it tonight."

Grinning at the bound boys, Mr. Harris turned
and walked from the cabin. In the silence, Bob and
Pete looked at each other helplessly. They could see
the sun low through one of the dirty windows of the
cabin. Night would soon be upon them, and they
could do nothing to stop Mr. Harris.

"We must be somewhere on the Sandow Estate,"
Pete said with his unerring sense of direction. "I
recognized some mountains when the truck stopped."

"If we could only have left a sign," Bob added, "but there wasn't any chance the way they hustled us into that truck."

"Jupiter'll find us. But if we could get loose first, maybe we could send out some signal." Pete began to strain at the bonds that tied his hands behind him.

There was a laugh of amusement. Mr. Harris had come back to the cabin again.

"Stout lads, eh? I truly admire your determination."

"You won't get away with this!" Pete said hotly.

Mr. Harris grinned. "By now, boys, the police and your friend Jupiter are looking high and low for those dark men who they fear have captured you. A most happy set of circumstances for me."

"Don't think you've fooled Jupiter!" Bob declared. "You'll go to prison."

"I think not," Mr. Harris said confidently. "I have planned too carefully to be stopped now by boys and small-town policemen. Still, you have caused me certain problems, and I would feel safer if I could persuade you to join my effort."

"We wouldn't join a man like you!" Pete declared stoutly.

"Bold words, but quite stupid. You should have made a deal, and then turned on me when you were free. It's lucky for me that most people are so stupid. Otherwise the Chumash Hoard would have been found long ago."

"I don't think you've really found it," Bob said.

"Wrong, my boy. I have solved Magnus Verde's little riddle, and in a few hours I shall have the Hoard," Mr. Harris declared, and his eyes narrowed as he looked at the boys. "At that time, I may return to deal with you two."

He turned and strode to the door. As he touched the knob, he looked over his shoulder. "By the way, it will do you no good to free yourselves. This cabin is at the edge of a sheer hundred foot drop. It can be reached only by way of a narrow cut, and I have a man on guard there. He has a clear view of the only door. There is no way off this little plateau."

With a sarcastic laugh, Mr. Harris left the cabin. This time the boys heard the lock turn. They were alone—locked in. Pete instantly began to struggle with his bonds again.

"Bob," Pete said, "maybe we could help each other. Can you roll over so that we're sitting back-to-back?"

The two investigators struggled across the rough floor until they were finally seated back-to-back. Pete began to struggle with the ropes on Bob's wrists. Sweat poured down his face, and he gritted his teeth. He worked for what seemed like hours, then slumped down exhausted.

"I just can't get enough grip," he said miserably.

"It's the way our hands are tied," Bob said.

Pete searched for a way. "If Mr. Harris hadn't

taken my knife, I could have held it in my teeth, and——"

"Teeth!" Bob exclaimed. "Maybe we can loosen the knots with our teeth."

"It's worth a try. I'll lie on my side."

Pete lay flat with his back to Bob. The smaller of the investigators inched up to Pete's wrists. His teeth took a strong grip on the first knot. Pete pulled against him, and Bob began to chew at the knot. Three times they had to stop and rest. Then Bob tried again.

"I can feel it opening!" Pete cried low. "Try with your hands now."

Back-to-back again, Bob's hands worked on Pete's ropes. Suddenly, the first knot came loose. The second knot was easier, and moments later Pete's hands were free. He quickly freed his legs, and then released Bob.

They immediately took stock of their situation. Pete went to the front windows, while Bob investigated the single rear window.

"The front windows are nailed shut," Pete reported, "and I can see the guard. We couldn't get out without being seen, even in the dark. He's got a big lantern."

Already the sun was down behind the highest peaks, and the land was turning a twilight purple. Darkness came early and fast in the mountains in winter.

"There's nothing back here except a few feet of ledge and then the cliff." Bob sounded discouraged. "I guess it's hopeless to try to get out."

The two investigators returned to the table in the middle of the room.

"At least I know where we are," Pete said. "I can see the pass to the west. We're about five miles from the big house, right in the high mountains."

"Maybe if we sent out a signal it would be seen at the house," Bob suggested. "If Jupiter is looking for us, he'd be sure to go to the house."

"Some kind of light," Pete decided.

They began to search the cabin. There did not seem to be much hope—the mountain cabin contained few furnishings, and Harris was a smart man. But, like many overconfident crooks, Harris had overlooked the obvious. Bob cried out in triumph as he unpiled debris from the lid of an old woodbin and opened the lid.

"Here's an oil lamp!" He pulled out the dusty old lamp. "It's got some kerosene in it! We can flash out a Morse code signal by covering and uncovering it. An SOS!"

"If we can light it," Pete pointed out. "We don't have any matches."

Frantically, the boys searched the cabin again. Once more they were in luck. They found an old book of matches tucked away in the table drawer. Bob grabbed one and quickly lighted the lantern,

while Pete got a flat piece of tin to cover the light and flash the signal. The boys started for the rear window.

They stopped, their mouths wide open in astonishment!

A dark face was peering in at them through the window.

The window was pulled open, and the two dark men in the strange white clothes climbed inside. They stood staring at the boys, their long knives gleaming in their hands.

A DEAD END

Chief Reynolds was at his desk when Jupiter and Worthington burst in. Jupiter waved the tell-tale sandwich wrapper.

"Mr. Harris is a fraud, sir!" Jupiter shouted. "He's trying to get the Hoard. We saw him driving away fast from his headquarters. I think he's gone to the Sandow Estate, and I'm sure he has Bob and Pete."

"Whoa, Jupiter. Let me see what you have." The Chief examined the stains on the wrapper. "So he's not even a vegetarian. The League is a fraud, too. Well, that fits."

Jupiter gaped. "Fits what, Chief?"

"What I've found out," the Chief said, and his eyes twinkled. "You boys aren't the only detectives in Rocky Beach. I have been talking to the authorities in Australia. They knew nothing about Ted

Sandow, but they did know an Albert Harris. Your hunch was right."

"What did you find out, sir?"

The Chief stood up. "I'll tell you as we go. There's no time to lose now. We haven't found a trace of the missing dark men, but I have a feeling that when we find Mr. Harris we'll find them. I've called Mr. Andrews, and we'll pick him up on our way. Pete's dad is away, unfortunately."

"Where are we going, Chief?" Jupiter wanted to know.

"Why, the Sandow Estate. I'm certain that you're right about that, too. That's where we'll find our villains."

"Perhaps we ought to take the Rolls-Royce, sir," Jupiter suggested. "Mr. Harris doesn't know we use it, and he might try to escape if he sees a police car."

"A good idea, Jupiter. I'll have my men come along behind in the police car."

The Chief ordered four men into the police car and instructed them to follow the Rolls-Royce but not too closely. Then Worthington drove Jupiter and the Chief to Bob's house. Mr. Andrews hurried out and climbed in.

"What's happening, Chief?" he asked in a worried voice. "Have you located Bob and Pete?"

"Not yet, Mr. Andrews, but we will," Chief Reynolds said.

"How did all this come about?" Mr. Andrews wanted to know.

Chief Reynolds quickly summed up all that had happened to The Three Investigators. "They've done good work, Mr. Andrews. You should be proud of them. Without them, Miss Sandow and Ted could be in grave trouble, and we wouldn't have known until too late. The boys acted well and carefully. They had no way of knowing about Harris. He fooled everyone."

"Just who is this Harris?" Mr. Andrews asked uneasily.

"A thief and a fraud, as Jupiter and the boys have shown," the Chief replied as Worthington drove up the winding road toward the pass in the fading twilight. "I just talked with the police in Sydney, Australia. Harris is a wanted man down there. He's a notorious confidence man, cat burglar, extortionist, and much more. He's often posed as the leader of some fake organization to fleece innocent people. He's even wanted in Mexico, where he operated a fraudulent scheme to aid poor Indians."

"Mexico, sir?" Jupiter said. "Was he there recently?"

"More than once, and the most recent visit was only a year or so ago. The Australians think he was also in California for a while less than a year ago."

"That must have been when he learned of the Chumash Hoard and Miss Sandow," Jupiter decided.

"I suspect that he read about her brother's death in one of the local papers," Chief Reynolds explained.

"That was probably how he came to seek out Ted Sandow in England."

They reached the top of the pass, with Worthington driving fast but with perfect control, and raced on in the dark night to the iron gates. The big gold car had long outdistanced the following police car. The gates were open. Worthington swung the car through them with scarcely a slackening in the pace of the powerful machine.

The great car roared on until Worthington brought it to a gentle stop at the front door of the big Spanish style house. They piled out quickly, and Chief Reynolds motioned everyone to silence. There were no lights on in the house, and no sign of life.

"It looks like no one's here," Chief Reynolds said in disappointment.

"They may have left some clue, though, as to where they went," Jupiter suggested.

"Let's take a look at least," Mr. Andrews urged. "Bob and Pete may be locked up somewhere inside."

Chief Reynolds nodded, and signaled to his men in the police car, which had just arrived and parked quietly some distance from the house. While the men spread out around the house, the Chief led Jupiter, Mr. Andrews and Worthington inside.

They searched all the downstairs rooms cautiously, but found nothing. Jupiter bit his lip in chagrin. Were they too late? Had Mr. Harris kidnapped everyone so he could hold them as hostages

until he got away with the Chumash Hoard? Then
Worthington spoke quietly:

"Gentlemen, I believe I hear something."

They all listened in the dark house.

Thump—thump—thump—thump!

"It's upstairs," Chief Reynolds said. "In the back!"

With the Chief leading the way, his pistol in hand,
they mounted the stairs carefully and went along the
second floor corridor toward the source of the banging.

Thump—thump—thump!

"In there," Mr. Andrews said, pointing to a door in
the left wall.

The door was locked. Chief Reynolds motioned
for them to stand back while he hurled his bulk
against the door. It cracked but did not break down.
The Chief battered it again, and it flew open. His
pistol ready, the Chief led the way into the room.

"There!" Mr. Andrews cried.

Something that looked like an Egyptian mummy
lay on the floor in a corner of the dark room, thump-
ing its legs against the wall. It was Ted Sandow
trussed up and gagged. They freed the English boy,
and he cried:

"Aunt Sarah! Over there!"

The frail little woman was tied firmly to a chair
with a gag in her mouth. Worthington released her,
and she stared with wide, shocked eyes at all of
them.

"I . . . I . . . what happened?" Her eyes were

dazed, confused. "I remember Mr. Harris bringing me my afternoon tea, and the next thing I knew I awakened here in this chair! My goodness, I've never been so frightened. And poor Theodore! On the floor!"

The fluttering little lady hurried to Ted and clucked over him like a hen. Ted smiled at her, then turned to Jupiter.

"After I left you in the library, Jupiter, I came back to find that both you and Mr. Harris were gone. He didn't return until late afternoon. He told me he had some important evidence about the amulet to show me upstairs. Naturally, I came up with him and suddenly he must have struck me on the head from behind. When I regained consciousness I was tied up like a mummy. I've been here ever since."

"Of course!" Jupiter was beginning to understand the whole plot. "When Mr. Harris and I came back from the lodge, he must have told me that you had driven off somewhere in order to make me suspicious. You hadn't gone out at all."

"It also gave Harris a chance to reach his office in time to abduct Bob and Pete," Chief Reynolds added. "Jupiter had told him that they would be there."

"Please," Jupiter groaned, "don't remind me. I told him everything, and he got us all out of the way!"

"He must be going for the Hoard tonight," Ted said. "I feel completely responsible. He wormed his way into my confidence to get here. All that about you boys being thieves, and the reward, was his idea. He suggested reaching you by offering the junk. He used me like a toy."

"Don't blame yourself, Theodore." Aunt Sarah tried to console him. "He took me in, too. I even donated money to his League. He had such fine letters of introduction from other vegetarians I know."

"Forged, I'm sure," Chief Reynolds said. "A tricky man."

"But we have to find him," Jupiter reminded them. "Ted, did he say anything to you about those dark men or the headless midgets?"

"Gosh, Jupiter, not that I remember."

Jupiter frowned. "I'm convinced that those headless-looking prisoners are the key. One of them must have stolen the amulet and thrown it over the wall with his message. Which means that they must be Yaquali Indians. But why does Harris have them?"

Mr. Andrews burst out, "Why are we worrying about amulets and midgets? It's Bob and Pete we have to think about now!"

"But we aren't likely to find them unless we find Harris," Chief Reynolds said.

The adults all looked at each other helplessly. Jupiter chewed on his lip. Suddenly, he turned to Miss Sandow:

"Ma'am, did your brother ever mention the

Chumash Hoard?"

"No. Mark was so young when he had to flee, poor boy."

"What did he tell you about those two amulets?"

"Nothing, Jupiter. He gave them to me just before he left and said that they were useless. He said he had killed his goose. I always wondered what he meant by that."

Jupiter blinked. "Why, he must have meant he had killed the goose that would have laid his golden egg! The man he killed must have known the secret of the Hoard. The amulets aren't clues at all. They just proved that there was a Hoard on the estate. That man knew where it was!"

"So Mark Sandow didn't know the secret," Chief Reynolds said. "Yet Harris must, but how?"

"He must have solved Magnus Verde's riddle," Jupiter declared. "Maybe those dark men told him. And now we have to solve it to find him."

"In the eye of the sky where no one can find it," Chief Reynolds recited. "What could it mean? Where do we look?"

No one answered. They all stared at each other.

"If we could only find those dark men."

Jupiter groaned, and the big house seemed to mock him with its silence.

DOWN THE CLIFF

The two dark-complexioned men stood menacingly in the mountain cabin, their long knives in their hands. As Bob and Pete backed slowly toward the wall, Pete clutched the lantern, ready to hurl it in self-defense if necessary.

One of the men shook his head at Pete, speaking in a harsh, guttural voice:

"No! You no understand. We friends. Come to help."

Bob stared. "You speak English?"

"Sí, a little. I Natches. This my brother Nanika."

"If you want to help, why did you steal the statuette?" Pete demanded hotly.

"We see you find little gold man on road. We think it holds words from our little brother, Vittorio. We follow you, take gold man, but no words in him."

"We kept the message," Pete blurted out.

"So?" Natches said. "What words tell?"

Pete told them the message, and Natches began to nod in excitement. The two dark men put their knives away.

"Is what we fear," Natches said. "Our little brother is in danger. This Harris liar, bad man!"

"You are Yaquali Indians from Mexico, aren't you?" Bob asked. "And Harris has your brother prisoner."

"Sí, yes," Natches said. "We come to find brother. We are afraid. We no like city. But we must find Vittorio and other boys."

"Why didn't you try to talk to us in English when you chased us?" Bob wanted to know.

"When excited, cannot remember the English," Natches explained sadly.

"Why does Harris have your brother? What is he doing?"

In halting English, Natches told his story.

A month ago Harris had come to the Yaquali village deep in the Sierra Madre Mountains of Mexico and offered to take four of their boys to America to perform climbing feats at a public amusement park. It seemed to be a good opportunity for the boys. Vittorio was one of them.

"We are poor," Natches said. "Our young boys must learn new ways. Mr. Harris tell us they will make much money, will see America."

Harris took the boys, and the village was happy. The boys would see a new world, and there would be money. Then, a week ago, a letter reached the village. It came from Rocky Beach and revealed that Vittorio needed help. Somehow, the boy had managed to get it mailed.

"We leave, get old car, come here," Natches went on. "We find Mr. Harris at fine *hacienda* in mountain. We think we hear Vittorio cry for help. We watch, see you find gold man. Next day we follow your big car—first to big studio, then to house where we get little man from you. When gold man not have letter from Vittorio inside, we look again for Mr. Harris. We find him in big house. Try to make him tell where are boys. He fights with us and calls police to put us in jail. We scared, run away."

"You mean Mr. Harris started the fight to get you arrested?" Bob began to understand.

"*Sí,*" Natches agreed. "So we watch more and next day see you boys come out of big house. We chase, but you fool us. We watch again, see Harris put two boys in truck. We follow to here, wait, climb cliff to talk with you. You tell us where Mr. Harris go now."

"We don't know," Pete said.

"What is he doing with your boys? Do you have any idea?" Bob asked.

"Some bad thing," Natches said grimly. "We

think he use boys for evil, then maybe kill them. They know what he do."

Pete exclaimed, "He must be using them to get the Hoard! They're expert climbers. And when he gets it, he sure won't want them around to tell about it."

"We've got to get out and call Chief Reynolds," Bob said.

"You wish to go out?" Natches said. "We go then."

"How? There's a guard out there, and we couldn't get near him," Pete explained.

"We go down cliff," Natches said simply.

Nanika nodded eagerly, gesturing at the rear window and pointing down—down the sheer cliff to the jagged rocks far below.

"Down the cliff?" Pete drew back from the window.

"There is no danger with us, *muchacho*."

Bob looked at Pete, then back at Natches. "We'll try it," he said. "It's the only chance we have."

"Let's send out some signals first," Pete said, resigned to this new danger.

He and Bob carried the lantern to the window, and with the help of the flat sheet of tin, sent out a series of SOS signals in Morse code. Then all four of them climbed through the window, and Natches and Nanika threw thin rawhide ropes down the face of the cliff. They wedged two thick wooden stakes into the rocks at the top and motioned to the boys.

"We have straps on chest and shoulders," Natches instructed. "You will grasp shoulder straps very tight, and climb on backs. That way we carry you down."

Pete clung to Natches, and Bob to Nanika. Then, without another word, the two Yaquali dropped over the edge of the cliff. Pete's head seemed to spin as he felt himself falling into space, and Bob clutched tightly to the straps on Nanika's back.

The two Yaquali bounced down the sheer cliff with the speed and agility of flies on a wall. They slid down the ropes, bouncing from rock wall to crevice as they descended swiftly and without pause. At times they swung far out into open space while Bob and Pete clung desperately to their backs. Then the two Indians would swing back to the cliff face at exactly the right spot to continue their unhindered descent. They went down the cliff face in the darkness as easily as other men walk a city street.

The boys hung tight, their eyes closed. It seemed as if the trip down would never end. At last they realized that the Indians were on flat ground again. Cautiously they lowered their legs and opened their eyes.

"We made it!" Bob cried in relief.

Natches grinned. "Is not so bad. That easy."

"Don't tell me about the hard ones then," Pete declared weakly. "But we better hurry. Where's your car, Natches?"

"Road to left. We go for police? They will help?"

"They sure will when we tell them what we know!" Bob declared.

They all hurried along a trail toward the place where Natches and Nanika had parked their old car.

Just as they reached the road, the bright lights of a truck flashed on, blinding them.

Mr. Harris stepped out of the shadows, holding a rifle. "You two boys are beginning to become tiresome. But at least you have brought me my Yaquali friends. I was just a little worried about them running loose."

"How . . ." Bob stammered, "how did you . . ."

"Find you? Simple, I saw your signals and came to investigate."

"Oh, no!" Pete groaned.

Mr. Harris laughed, turning to speak to his burly assistant, Sanders, who stood behind him with another rifle. In that instant, Nanika muttered something and leaped at Mr. Harris. The fake vegetarian stepped adroitly aside, striking Nanika on the head. The Indian fell to the dirt and lay there, motionless.

"Mr. Harris!" Sanders cried. "The other one!"

Harris whirled, but Natches had vanished into the night. He was nowhere to be seen. Mr. Harris glared furiously at the boys. His confident manner vanished for a moment. Then the thief and confidence man laughed coldly.

"No matter, let him go. We'll soon be far away and one missing Indian won't bother us."

Sanders looked uneasy. "You sure, boss?"

"Of course I'm sure, you idiot! Go and get Carson from his post in front of the cabin. We'll have to take these meddling fools with us. I'm tired of them bothering me. We'll put an end to that!"

Sanders went off into the night. Nanika still lay silent on the ground, and Mr. Harris continued to glare at Bob and Pete. In sudden fear, they realized that this time they could not get away.

INTO THE MOUNTAINS

In front of the big Spanish estate house, Chief Reynolds returned from the police car. "No report on those dark men or their car. I'm sorry, Mr. Andrews. But we'll think of some way to find them."

"How?" Bob's dad said nervously. "We don't have any idea where they are. We've found no trace of them!"

They were all out in front of the house where the moonlight turned all the shadows into silver ghosts. Jupiter paced up and down, his round face looking like a miniature owl deep in thought.

"Chief, we do have some idea where they are, I think," he said slowly. "First, the Hoard must be in the mountains on the estate somewhere. Second, Mr. Harris has a car and a truck. Third, it's almost certain he plans to get the Hoard tonight. His various ruses to get us out of the way were not designed to hold us for long, just to delay us."

"But how does all that help us, Jupiter?" Ted said, puzzled.

"It means that he is planning to use a road, and the road is almost certainly on the estate. It probably goes into the mountains, and isn't very far from here," Jupiter explained eagerly. "We can rule out the road to the house, and the road to the lodge. So what other roads are there? . . . Miss Sandow can tell us."

"By golly, Jupiter, I think you're right," said Chief Reynolds.

The Chief turned to Aunt Sarah, while Mr. Andrews, Ted and Worthington all stared out into the night toward the eastern mountains.

"What other roads are there, Miss Sandow?" Chief Reynolds asked.

"Well," the fragile, little lady said, blinking her eyes as she thought, "I haven't been around the estate much in recent years, but——"

Ted suddenly interrupted, "Look! Over there! A light, see? It's flashing."

They all looked toward the mountains. No one breathed. They waited. Then the faint point of light flashed again—low in the sky, just above the nearest trees.

"It's an SOS!" Jupiter cried. "I bet it's Bob and Pete. They're probably being held prisoner up there."

"About five miles away, I'd say," Chief Reynolds said. "And just about where the foothills of the high mountains begin."

"Due east, also, Chief," Worthington pointed out.

The pinpoint of light flashed once more.

"What is out there, Miss Sandow?" Jupiter asked excitedly.

"Why, I'm not sure," Aunt Sarah said. "It's been so long. Wait now, yes, my father had an old cabin on the east range. My goodness, I'd forgotten all about that. No one goes out there any more."

"How do we reach it, ma'am?" asked Mr. Andrews.

"Well, there is a road— rather narrow. It goes on into the high mountains. The road runs just below the cabin. You see, it's built on a mesa on top of a cliff. It's quite hard to reach."

"Just where Mr. Harris would hold prisoners," Jupiter observed.

They all stared in the direction of the light, but it did not flash again. Though they waited expectantly, there were no more signals.

"Something must have happened." Mr. Andrews looked worried.

"Let's head for that cabin," Chief Reynolds said grimly. "There's no time to lose."

The Rolls-Royce led the way with Jupiter, Chief Reynolds, Ted and Mr. Andrews in the back seat. The police car came behind, carrying the Chief's men, except for one who was left behind to guard Miss Sandow. They raced along the highway until they reached the dirt side road described by Miss Sandow.

As they entered the mountain road, they turned out their lights. In the dark they had to proceed more slowly, though the moonlight outlined everything in its ghostly glow. Soon they were at the very bottom of the towering mountains. Both cars drew to a stop and everyone got out.

Jupiter pointed upward to where a small cabin was clearly visible, bathed in moonlight and nestled on a kind of mesa.

"There it is!"

"There's no light now," Mr. Andrews whispered.

"We'll work our way up carefully. It could be a trap," Chief Reynolds said.

"Hurry, Chief. Bob and Pete may be in immediate danger," Mr. Andrews said urgently.

"They may be in worse danger if we're spotted too soon," the Chief pointed out. "Stay back, Jupiter. Harris is a dangerous man."

Jupiter nodded reluctantly, and stayed behind as the Chief and his men started up the steep, narrow path that led up to the mesa. A sudden commotion to the right made them all stop. Worthington and Mr. Andrews, who had been standing near the Rolls-Royce, were struggling with a short, powerful man.

"The dark men!" Jupiter cried.

"Bring him here, men!" Chief Reynolds commanded his policemen.

Two of the policemen joined Worthington and Mr. Andrews and dragged the struggling Natches to where the Chief and Jupiter were waiting. When the Yaquali saw Jupiter, he stopped struggling, and an eager smile spread across his dark face.

"You Jupiter, no? I Natches. Friend. Yaquali friend. I escape."

"We'll decide if you're a friend," Chief Reynolds said ominously. "You attacked these boys?"

"*Sí*. Mistake. I think they *amigos* of bad man Harris. I am wrong, tell other boys. They believe."

"You've seen Bob and Pete?" Mr. Andrews cried. "Where are they? Tell us!"

Natches looked around in despair. "Evil one— Harris—take them. My brother Nanika, too. Already have little brother Vittorio prisoner. I escape."

Chief Reynolds sighed. "You better start at the beginning and explain just what this is all about."

"Just a minute, Chief," Jupiter interrupted. "I bet they speak Spanish. . . . Do you?" he asked, turning toward Natches.

The Indian nodded eagerly.

"Then tell us in Spanish," Jupiter said. "Both Chief Reynolds and I can understand it."

Natches started to tell his story again. But this time he could tell it much faster. They all listened closely, expressing considerable indignation over the treacherous Harris.

"You say he has four of your boys?" Jupiter asked. "Of course! I've been very dumb. He's using Yaquali boys. It's the answer to Magnus Verde's riddle. And all the time *we've* been saying that his words were, 'It's in the eye of the sky where no one can find it.' "

"Well, *wasn't* that his message?" Chief Reynolds asked.

"No, sir, it wasn't. His words were, 'It's in the eye of the sky where no *man* can find it.' No *man,* you see. He meant that no man could find it, but a boy could!"

"A boy!" Chief Reynolds exclaimed.

"Exactly, sir. Indians are small, and in those days they were smaller. Magnus Verde's band hid their Hoard where only a boy could get to it. Some cave with a very narrow opening."

"You mean that Harris figured out the true meaning and went to the Yaquali village to get four boys who would be small enough to make the climb and get into the cave?"

"That's right," Jupiter said. "He knew they were expert climbers."

"That means it's up high somewhere," the Chief analyzed, shaking his head. "But I don't know why that narrow opening would stop him. He could drill the entrance larger, or dynamite it."

"No, I don't think so," Jupiter said. "In the first place that might collapse the cave and bury the gold forever. In the second place Harris is trying to steal the Hoard. He couldn't risk drilling or blasting right out in the open."

Mr. Andrews interrupted. "Can't we figure it out later? Right now the important thing is to rescue the boys. Do you know where Harris took them, Natches?"

Natches pointed along the road toward the higher mountains. "That way. On road in truck."

"That's deep into the mountains," Chief Reynolds said. "We could look for days. If we wait till morning we can get helicopters."

"Morning could be too late!" Mr. Andrews cried.

"We can't just blunder around, Mr. Andrews. That could endanger the boys' lives more."

Jupiter had been silent during the discussion. Suddenly he turned to Natches. "Mr. Natches, can you track them?"

"Track?" Natches said. "*Sí*, of course. I track easy."

Chief Reynolds cried, "Come on, then! I only hope we're in time."

Natches began to trot along the road in the moonlight. The others followed in silence.

Mr. Harris stood beside Bob and Pete in a desolate canyon deep in the moonlit mountains. Both boys had been securely tied with heavy ropes.

"Fools! I should have dealt with you at once. Well, it won't be long now."

Sanders appeared quietly from the shadows.

"The Yaqualis are ready, boss."

"Good," Harris said. "That fat friend of these fools is undoubtedly raising a hue and cry right now. It isn't wise to underestimate him. He's a clever boy. We must work fast. Follow me, Sanders."

Bob and Pete watched the two villains fade into the silver shadows of the box-like canyon. To their left, Nanika groaned weakly where he lay trussed hand and foot.

"What do we do now?" Pete asked.

"I hope Harris is right, and Jupe is looking for us."

"Maybe he saw our signal."

"We didn't have much time to send it," Bob said without too much hope. "And even if he saw it he'd go to the cabin. How will they ever find us in the dark?"

"I don't know, but they better," Pete said. "I've got a hunch we won't be around by daylight!"

Before Bob could answer, Harris and Sanders reappeared. The fake vegetarian seemed pleased with himself. He nodded to Sanders, who bent down and untied Bob.

"Up with you," Harris snapped at Bob. "Sanders, you're sure you know what to do?"

"I know, boss."

"Good. This should take no more than a few hours with the four boys working. Be alert, Sanders. We've almost got the Hoard."

Harris pushed Bob before him, and together they vanished into the night up the canyon. Pete stared after them with an uneasy feeling. Why had Harris taken Bob with him?

Pete had a vague idea where they were. Although the deep box canyon had no name, it was at the base of the towering bulk of Indian Head Mountain, deep in the mountains at the edge of the Sandow Estate. The road and the truck were more than a mile away. How would anyone ever find them?

"Sanders?" Pete said. "Harris will leave you . . ."

"You be quiet," Sanders growled. "The boss knows what he's doing."

Pete lapsed into a defeated silence. The injured Nanika moved and struggled up to a sitting position. The broad, powerful Yaquali looked around wildly. Pete tried to smile reassuringly at Nanika, but he could say nothing. The Indian spoke no English. If Pete was to do anything, he would have to do it alone.

But what could he do? Sanders sat only a few feet away, holding a rifle and watching the two prisoners intently. Pete stared all around, looking desperately for some clue that would suggest a possible course of action.

Suddenly he blinked. He must be seeing things!
Shadowy figures seemed to be rising up all around
the small canyon. He shouted:

"Here I am! Help! We're here!"

The figures all began to run toward him. Sanders
jumped up, looked frantically at the men rushing
toward him, and then dropped his rifle and ran into
the darkness.

"Get that man!" Chief Reynolds cried.

Moments later Jupiter, Mr. Andrews and Worthington were crowding around Pete, trying to untie
the ropes. Natches ran to Nanika and quickly untied his brother. Two of Chief Reynolds' men came
back with Sanders, who was still struggling to get
away.

"Where's Mr. Harris?" Jupiter asked Pete.

"He went up the canyon toward Indian Head
Mountain," Pete said, "and he's got Bob with
him!"

Mr. Andrews looked despairing. "He still has
Bob?"

Chief Reynolds glared at the surly-looking Sanders. "Where is Harris, you! What's he done with
Bob and those Indian boys?"

"Why don't you just find out, cop," Sanders
sneered.

"There's another man, too," Pete said. "A fellow
named Carson."

"Well, they won't get away," the Chief said.

"They're trapped. This is a box canyon! It's all over."

Sanders looked scornful. "Don't think you got the boss beat yet, cop."

"He can't be far away," said Pete. "He's up the canyon, and it doesn't go in too far, Chief."

"He can't get out any way but through us," Jupiter pointed out.

"Right," Chief Reynolds agreed. "Okay, men, spread out and move up the canyon."

The group spread out, their guns ready, and advanced alertly up the canyon toward Indian Head Mountain. The mountain towered pale and silvery in the moonlight.

As the canyon gradually narrowed in the shadowy light, they continued to move ahead. Aware that the Hoard was probably somewhere high up, they kept glancing up toward the mountaintop as they advanced. Jupiter, in the rear with Pete and Worthington, suddenly exclaimed as he stared up at the bulk of the mountain against the moonlight.

"Pete! The mountain! See, it——"

He got no farther. From the silver shadows of the canyon the wild, insane laugh burst out, bouncing and echoing from the walls of the canyon.

"The laughing shadow!" Pete cried.

"Over there!" Chief Reynolds yelled. "Shine your lights!"

The police aimed their flashlights into the shadows.

Mr. Harris stood there, smiling.

"Well, you arrived a little too early," he said. "Unfortunate. Now I shall have to settle for less than I wanted, eh?"

From nearby the crazy laugh rang out again, drowning out the rest of Harris' words.

THE CHUMASH HOARD!

"Don't move, Harris!" Chief Reynolds ordered. "Take him, men, and search him. Where's the other man?"

A policeman called from the dark, "We've got him, sir!"

Harris stood smiling while he was searched. A policeman took a small sack from him, and handed it to the Chief. The assistant, Carson, was hustled to stand beside Harris. Chief Reynolds opened the bag, and faced the smiling criminal.

"There's gold in the bag, Harris, which means you've found the Hoard. You better tell us where it is. We know all about you."

"All about me?" Harris smiled. "I doubt that.

Those dirty Indians may have told you some story, but you can't believe——"

"I've also talked to Australia," the Chief interrupted him.

Harris paled. "Australia? But how did you find out?"

"Jupiter, tell him . . ." the Chief began, but before he could finish his sentence, a huge bird swooped down out of the dark, flew straight to Mr. Harris and perched on his head. It was a large, shaggy bird about the size of a crow, with a very big, long, black-and-yellow beak, a ragged brownish crest, a white chest and belly, and a ragged tail. Its body was thick, and its head seemed too big for its size.

"What is that?" Pete asked, staring at the odd bird.

Before anyone could answer, it opened its enormous beak and let out a wild, crazy laugh that seemed to fill the whole canyon.

"The laugh!" Pete yelled "It was a bird!"

"A *kookaburra* bird, to be exact," Jupiter announced, looking remarkably unsurprised. "Known in Australia as a Laughing Jackass. It's the thing I couldn't remember—an Australian animal with an almost human laugh."

Jupiter took a flashlight and aimed it at Mr. Harris. With the bird perched on his head, Harris cast a tall, humpbacked shadow with a birdlike head and beak that jerked and moved about.

"That's our laughing shadow," Jupiter said. "Mr. Harris with his pet kookaburra on his head—and the kookaburra is found only in Australia."

Mr. Harris nodded, and shrugged. "So, it was you who tripped me up, Jupiter? I was afraid something like this might happen, and I tried to get rid of the bird. Unfortunately, it stayed on the estate and kept crying out at awkward moments."

"Jupiter also spotted your meat sandwich, Harris," Chief Reynolds said. "You were careless."

"Ah, that too, eh? I should have dealt more firmly with our stout friend. However, as they say, all is not lost. I presume that you would like young Bob and the Indian boys back safely?"

Mr. Andrews cried, "What have you done with Bob?"

"Don't try anything, Harris," Chief Reynolds snapped. "You're in trouble enough."

"Too much trouble, Chief. However, I have my way out. It pays to be prepared," Harris said with a wicked smile. "Now, in that sack you took there is some gold. Not nearly as much as I had hoped to have, but a fair amount. I am willing to trade for it. I will take that gold, no more, and my freedom. You may keep Sanders and Carson to make it look good."

"Why you!" Sanders muttered, and lunged at his boss, but the police held him back.

"Tut, tut, Sanders, we must all look out for ourselves, eh? I can't be greedy. I'll trade myself and this gold for the boys and the rest of the treasure."

"No deals, Harris," Chief Reynolds declared. "We'll find the boys. You can't hurt them now that we have you and your men."

"On the contrary, Chief," Harris said smoothly. "You see, I prepared for this emergency. The boys are still beyond your reach unless I tell you where they are."

Chief Reynolds said, "Harris, I warn you that——"

"No!" Harris snapped, his voice harsh now. "I warn you! Unless you give me the gold, and my freedom, you will never find those boys alive! They cannot escape, and they cannot call for help. They have no food or water. If you let me go with that gold, I will telephone when I am clear and tell you where they are. Otherwise, they will die."

"You wouldn't dare! Why, that would be murder!"

Harris smiled. "Perhaps I wouldn't dare, but you can't be sure, can you? You have no choice!"

Harris' own laugh was low in the night. But his pet kookaburra echoed wildly from his perch on the criminal's head, and the high laughter filled the dark canyon. Mr. Andrews looked pleadingly at Chief Reynolds. Everyone else stared at the grinning Harris. Then Jupiter spoke up.

"No," he said quietly, "I think we do have a choice. Chief, I am sure I know where the boys are."

Harris turned his cold eyes toward Jupiter. Chief Reynolds looked doubtful.

"Where, Jupiter?" Mr. Andrews cried.

"Up there," Jupiter announced, and pointed to the black mountain towering above them. "Magnus Verde's words were, 'It is in the eye of the sky where no man can find it.' We know he was being tricky about saying no *man,* but I think he was telling the exact truth about the eye of the sky. He didn't mean the sun or the moon or anything *like* an eye. He meant a real eye. There, up on the mountain. Indian Head Mountain!"

Everyone looked upward. Etched against the silvery moonlit sky was a face. A giant rock face with a nose, mouth, and two eyes.

"The left eye is deep in shadows," Jupiter went on. "I think there's a ledge up there, and a cave. And that's where the Chumash Hoard is hidden. Harris must have been up there, too, and when he saw our lights down here he pushed the boys inside and sealed up the opening so they're trapped."

Harris muttered, "You think I can climb up there?"

Jupiter nodded. "With the help of the Yaquali boys, yes. The Australian police told us you had been a cat burglar."

"Suppose they *are* there, what can you do?"

"Natches and Nanika can get up there," Jupiter said.

Natches nodded eagerly. *"Sí!* We climb easy. *Mucho* easy."

"Are you going to listen to a kid?" Harris demanded of the adults. "I warn you, if you listen to him, and he's wrong, the whole deal is off! We deal now, or never."

The adults stood uneasily. Harris muttered an oath. Everyone looked at Mr. Andrews and the two Yaquali. Mr. Andrews spoke first:

"I'll trust Jupiter's hunch," he said. The two Indians nodded.

"All right," Chief Reynolds said, "Natches and Nanika can go up and look. But what if Harris has the boys tied up? If the cave opening is so small, Natches and Nanika may not be able to get inside."

"I don't see how Harris could have gotten inside to tie them," Jupiter replied. "Unless he had one boy tie all the others, and then tied him up and pushed him inside before sealing the cave. But I don't believe he had time to do that. However, perhaps I'd better go up, too, just in case. I might be able to get inside."

"You, Jupiter?" Chief Reynolds said, looking at the First Investigator's sturdy frame.

"Perdone," Natches said, "I do not think Jupiter he can make the climb. He is, yes, too big?"

Jupiter flushed at this reference to his size, but he reluctantly agreed. "I guess Pete will have to go."

"*Sí,*" Natches agreed. "Strong boy. Tall, not so heavy. He may get inside."

Pete gulped, "Yeh, I guess it's me."

Chief Reynolds herded Harris and his two glowering henchmen into a space between boulders, where they sat sullen and silent while Pete and the two Yaquali prepared for the climb. When they had their equipment ready, the Yaquali roped Pete between them and started up with Nanika in the lead.

From the floor of the dark canyon, the watchers saw them swarm up the cliff face like insects. They mounted rapidly and surely. It was obvious that without Pete the two Yaquali could have climbed the mountain as fast as they walked a street. But they guided the strong boy carefully and slowly.

On they went, upward, and at last they reached the ledge in the eye of the stone face. For a moment they paused at the shadowed ledge, and then they vanished over the edge.

"They made it!" Chief Reynolds cried below.

"With Natches and Nanika, there was no danger, sir," Jupiter observed. "Now they are in the eye of the sky."

High on the ledge, Pete and the two Yaquali saw a large boulder set against the rear wall deep inside

the stone eye. On the ledge there was a small pile of gold and a long iron bar.

"Jupe was right!" Pete cried. "This is where the gold is, and Harris used that iron bar to lever the boulder into the cave mouth. Come on, Natches."

They rolled the boulder away using the lever. Behind the boulder there was a small, dark hole in the cliff. It was far too small for the broad shoulders of Natches and Nanika. Pete took a flashlight.

"Tie a rope around my foot. If I signal, pull me out."

He crawled into the dark opening. He just barely squeezed through the narrow tunnel, forcing his way forward. Soon he sensed space ahead and a movement of air. He started to crawl faster—but stuck fast.

Though he struggled to move ahead, he could make no headway. He was too big to move another inch. He heard a sudden noise to his left and ahead. In panic, he switched on his flashlight and saw a figure with a large rock in its hand ready to hit him.

"Bob!" he cried.

"Pete!" Bob grinned. "Boy, am I glad to see you. I tried to tell the boys you'd all come for us, but I don't think they understood." Bob laughed, a little nervously. "You sure look funny stuck there. I barely got through myself."

Pete moved his flashlight around and saw that he was two feet short of the cave itself. Then he shifted the light again and the beam fell on four small, dark boys who were standing near Bob, grinning at him.

"Shine it farther back," Bob said.

Pete aimed the light at the rear of the small cave. "Wow!" he cried.

All across the rear of the cave, piled in mounds, spilling everywhere, was a vast, shining mass of gold and glowing jewels. The gold was of every possible shape, gleaming and sparkling in the beam of light. The jewels were every color of the rainbow, dazzling and glistening in a riot of color.

"The Chumash Hoard!" Pete cried, amazed. "We found it!"

ALFRED HITCHCOCK
DETECTS A LOOSE END

Alfred Hitchcock beamed at The Three Investigators as they sat in his office the next afternoon.

"So, the Chumash Hoard was indeed 'In the eye of the sky where no man could find it!' Old Magnus Verde told the exact truth, and therefore fooled everyone for two hundred years."

"No one thought about him telling the truth," Jupiter agreed.

"Until you boys came along!" The famous director looked pleased. "Well, your Mr. Harris and his henchmen will have much time to regret their devious ways."

"And when they get out of our jail, the Australians want them," Bob said.

"Their future is not bright," Mr. Hitchcock said

drily. "Did they confess all their nefarious actions?"

"Yes, sir," Pete said. "Mr. Harris was a very smart man. He heard about the legend of the Hoard and figured out the answer to Magnus Verde's riddle. But after he spotted Indian Head Mountain and found the cave, he couldn't get inside. He'd been at the Yaquali village while he was in Mexico, so he went down to get some Indian boys to climb for the gold."

Bob added, "He's admitted that he didn't want any American boys because he planned to do away with them afterwards. He was sure that four boys from a remote Indian village in Mexico would never be traced to him."

The famous director scowled. "A complete villain! You boys have done well to stop his black career."

"But," Jupiter took up the story, "the little brother of Natches and Nanika understands a little English, and he overheard Harris talking. He realized that Harris had some crime in mind and was going to dispose of the boys later. So he wrote a letter, and managed to toss it out of the truck. Luckily, someone found it and mailed it."

"The factor of fortune—chance!" Mr. Hitchcock pointed out. "Never underestimate it, my boys. It operates in all human actions. We'll never know who that unknown person was who mailed the letter, but he certainly saved those boys."

"Yes, sir, he did," Jupiter agreed.

"I wonder about one aspect of the affair," the famous director mused. "Harris seems to have delayed a long time before making his move to steal the Hoard."

Jupiter nodded, "Yes, he did. That was because he knew that it would be best if he could get the Hoard totally unseen. He didn't want anyone to know he had it. So he was waiting until he could get Ted and Miss Sandow off the estate. He was all ready to persuade them to go to a vegetarian meeting in San Francisco the very day we found the amulet. As soon as they were gone, he was going to get the Hoard, dispose of the boys, and escape in a private plane he had engaged. If it had worked, no one would ever have known he had the Hoard, or that it even existed, and he would be safe in South America."

Pete took up the story: "Only they took little Vittorio out to the cabin by himself one afternoon and he escaped. He was lurking around Miss Sandow's house when he spied the amulet through the library window. He stole it because he thought the gold might be useful."

"It *was* useful, too," Bob broke in, "but not because of the gold. He discovered the secret compartment and hid a message for help in it."

"Later he was caught," Pete interrupted again, "and that was the cry for help we heard. Vittorio hoped his brothers would find his note, but we found it instead."

"And fortunate it was!" said Mr. Hitchcock. "You boys solved the mystery well with little to go on. Tell me, were those amulets clues to the Hoard?"

"No, sir," Jupiter explained, "except that they proved there really was a Hoard. Of course, Natches wanted the first amulet because he thought it might have come from Vittorio. I'm afraid I committed a grave error about the second amulet, and Mr. Harris led me on. Everything he told me was a lie."

"An error, young Jones?" Mr. Hitchcock said, eyebrows raised.

"Yes, sir," Jupiter admitted sadly. "I assumed that Ted was guilty and the amulets were clues. That blinded me to the truth. It also made it easy for Mr. Harris to fool us. He simply encouraged me to continue believing what I had already assumed was true."

The famous director nodded slowly. "Yes, that is the worst error an investigator can make—assuming something to be true before it is proven. An open mind, always, that is the only way to escape being fooled. Now, explain one more point, young man. What caused you to realize that the laughing shadow was a kookaburra bird, and thus led you to Harris' Australian origin?"

"Well, of course, I was still fooled at the time, and thought the shadow was Ted. But his accent reminded me that there are British-type accents that don't come from England."

"Yes, I see that," Mr. Hitchcock agreed. "But what led you to the kookaburra and Australia in particular?"

Jupiter grinned. "It was the way no one could agree on what the shadow sounded like when it laughed. We all heard it differently. I remembered Edgar Allan Poe's famous story, 'The Murders in the Rue Morgue,' and . . ."

"Thunderation, of course! In that story no one could agree on what language the unseen murderer had been heard to speak. *None* of them could recognize the speech—because the murderer was an ape and was speaking no language at all!"

"Exactly, sir." Jupiter looked pleased with himself. "I suddenly thought that perhaps the laugh wasn't from a person at all. That's when I remembered an Australian animal that laughed. At first I couldn't remember exactly what animal, but when the bird came flying out of the dark I suddenly remembered the kookaburra bird."

Mr. Hitchcock laughed. "Splendid! The Laughing Jackass had the final merriment at Mr. Harris' expense. Ah, the sight of that Hoard must have been magnificent."

"It was, sir," Bob agreed, "and we've brought you a piece." He laid a dazzling gold goblet on the desk. "With Miss Sandow's compliments, sir."

"Thank the good lady, lads. This will join my growing collection of mementoes of your exploits. Now, what of the rest of the treasure. It belongs, I suppose, to Miss Sandow."

Pete said, "Professor Meeker is studying it. I believe the State has to determine its final disposition. Museums are eager to have pieces for their displays."

"Miss Sanders hopes that the Indians will realize some benefit from it," Bob added. "It would be nice if the Yaqualis could take some money back to their village."

Mr. Hitchcock nodded. "So the case ends. But, my young friends, I fear it is not complete. I detect a loose end."

"A loose end?" Pete exclaimed.

Jupiter was baffled. "I can't think what, sir?"

"Unless I missed something in your report, E. Skinner Norris is still to be dealt with."

The boys grinned.

"Never fear," said Jupiter. "We have plans for him."

And on that ominous note the case was concluded.

**ALFRED HITCHCOCK and the
Three Investigators Series**

The Secret of Terror Castle
The Mystery of the Stuttering Parrot
The Mystery of the Whispering Mummy
The Mystery of the Green Ghost
The Mystery of the Vanishing Treasure
The Secret of Skeleton Island
The Mystery of the Fiery Eye
The Mystery of the Silver Spider
The Mystery of the Screaming Clock
The Mystery of the Moaning Cave
The Mystery of the Talking Skull
The Mystery of the Laughing Shadow

DATE DUE

DATE DUE			
SEP 25			
FEB 5			
MAR 26			
OCT 8			
NOV 6			
MAR 21			
FEB 17			
MAY 5			
MAY 23			
MAY 21 1996			
GAYLORD			PRINTED IN U.S.A.